Evening Under Lamplight

David Campbell was born in 1915 in a brass bedstead on a sheep station near Adelong, New South Wales. He was educated in Australia and then at Cambridge, where he graduated in Arts. During World War II he was a pilot in the RAAF and was awarded the DFC and bar. He then lived on various properties near Canberra, farming and writing poetry, until his death in 1979.

David Campbell is regarded as one of Australia's finest lyric poets and received numerous awards for his work, including the second Patrick White Award in 1975, the Henry Lawson Australian Arts Award in 1970, plus the New South Wales Premier's Award and the Fellowship of Australian Writers' Christopher Brennan Award in 1980.

Evening Under Lamplight

Selected Stories of
David Campbell

with a foreword by
David Malouf

University of Queensland Press
ST LUCIA • LONDON • NEW YORK

This edition first published 1976 under the title *Flame and Shadow*
by University of Queensland Press
Box 42, St Lucia, Queensland, Australia
Reprinted 1987

Typeset by University of Queensland Press
Printed in Australia by The Australian Print Group, Maryborough

Distributed in the UK and Europe by University of Queensland Press
Dunhams Lane, Letchworth, Herts. SG6 1LF England

Distributed in the USA and Canada by University of Queensland Press
250 Commercial Street, Manchester, NH 03101 USA

Acknowledgment is made to Patrick White for his kind permission to use
an extract from *The Aunt's Story*

Cataloguing in Publication Data

National Library of Australia

Campbell, David, 1915–1979.
    Evening under lamplight.

    I. Title. II. Title: Flame and shadow.

A823'.3

British Library (data available)

Library of Congress (data applied for)

ISBN 0 7022 2106 6

Contents

Contents

Foreword

David Campbell was one of our finest lyric poets. That alone should guarantee the interest of these stories.

Critics, whose task it is to describe and make distinctions, find it useful to speak of poetry and prose as if they belonged to separate categories. A writer in his daily practice sees it otherwise. For him writing is a place of intersections. There are points in a poet's writing life when the interesting intersection between his own experience and the more open textures of prose is just where his spirit is most fully engaged, and where he wants for a time to work.

There is nothing odd about this. When a poet like David Campbell takes up his pen and observes the need to bring his world yet again to the page, he will not be intimidated by the formal difference, let us say, between descriptive sketch and lyric, or the adjustment that may be necessary in his language to relax its rhythms to the leaner but tougher lineaments of prose. What will sustain him is the assurance that it is the same world he is moving in and that he, however different the demands of the medium, is the same man, bringing with him the same sensory equipment, the same eye and ear for things, the same peculiar way of receiving and transforming reality that amounts, once he has got it down, to a created universe. Which is to say that David Campbell is as fully present in these fictional pieces as in the lightest and most profound of his lyrics. We recognize immediately the *feel* of his world, the mind, the landscape, the easy balance of masculine strength and grace, the precision, the delicacy, the humour — most of

all that characteristic inwardness that while making no
claims for itself goes straight to the heart of things.

All writing is one. These stories of growing up in the
Monaro and of life in the air force in World War II have
their own value as records of experience and create their
own insights, but have the added interest of standing at an
angle to another and greater body of work: the poems.

David Malouf,
Sydney, 1987

Evening Under Lamplight

to John and Raina

Ah! que le monde est grand à la clarté des lampes!
Aux yeux du souvenir que le monde est petit!

Baudelaire

Come On, Billy

I

When horses gallop at night, the sound is mysterious. There was Billy, frowzy with sleep, ambling through silence downhill on a drooping nighthorse. The frost, after a week of rain, had sharpened the hoof-falls. The horse's paunch creaked, and Billy was aware of the silence. He was aware of the cemetery on the dark ridge where the owls moped.

The pace of the nighthorse quickened, and he rode rigid. And to his heart-beats the horses were suddenly galloping. They crossed the fearful landscape of an earlier dawn. Billy whooped to his courage, and his whip sang in the frost.

Up the hard road he chased his phantoms, neck and neck with fear. But the old mare was a stayer, and on the hill-crest day was breaking. Serpent-heads tossed in the first light; a breakaway gelding bucked, down the skyline; but the mob came in to the whip. In the heavy stockyard the horses stood steaming, hock-deep in mud.

Billy's flat hand clapped the mare's withers. Hobbled, she browsed a stubble of frost. The rabbiting-pack yelled, leaping like lions up the wire net of their yard. And slowly the morning came over Bald Hill, whistling a tune of birds. The great clatter sent the

3

ghosts packing, and here were the stockmen to daunt them.

"Morning, Billy. Morning, Billy."

Billy, shy and proud, stood astride like his father, glad to be part of the morning bustle. Dogs snuffed for rats between the slabs of the stalls; horses were led out from the yard and saddled up; in twos and threes the men rode off to work between the misty gum-trees. The smell of their tobacco-smoke remained. And, to forget a sudden sadness, Billy turned and ran a hard race down the rutted road to the homestead.

II

"And I wasn't frightened, neither."

Lined with porridge and cream and the fat meat of chops, Billy could taunt his sister and any old ghost.

"It was easy," he said. "While Len's sick, I'll get the horses in every morning. You're only a girl."

"I'm older than you are."

"That doesn't count."

But Janet only smiled. Her blue eyes were in their corners and she looked far away. Her indifference was elaborate, her smile mocked in secret.

"Let's go to dad's office and squash flies," she said.

The office was a dark high room in the old part of the house. A giant roll-top desk stood open in the light from the one window, where dead fingers of vine gripped the gauze. A few early blowflies staggered up the panes. They were easy to catch, and made a fine mess when slammed in a ledger.

The fair heads touched. And "Ach!" said Billy, twisting his neck and screwing up his face, eyeing the open page obliquely with the pleasure of disgust. "Just look at that one, Jan."

The fly had spread out like a blot over the neat figures.

Janet puckered an angel's nose, and her eyes were wide and bright. But she turned to trace a signature cut sharply in the glass pane.

"A.G. Wise," she spelt out at length. "Know who he was?"

"Of course." Billy was busy.

"He went mad and cut his name in the pane with a diamond ring."

"I know," said Billy, loud with impatience. "I know."

"Look, Billy, feel it. Give me your finger. He died and he's buried over in the cemetery. He must have been a silly old man, don't you think?"

"I know all that," Billy said. "I knew all that before you did. He buried his fortune at the front gate."

"He must have been a silly old man." And then, in joyous fright, "Look out, here comes the Doctor!"

Janet slipped like a slim wind over the sill and under the swinging gauze. Her head bobbed once, and was gone, leaving Billy in panic in the dim office, holding the ledger.

Clop, clop, clop!

Doctor Dalrymple's steady footsteps rang on the verandah. So Billy walked when he thought of it, firmly, in meditation, aping the big man he feared. But this was no time for laughter; he was trapped. He ran to the window, papers blew about him in the draught. He grabbed at them, listened, and dived to crouch in the knee-cavity of the desk.

Clop! and the window banged down. He could see

his father's tan boots amongst the papers, and, hugging the tell-tale ledger, he prayed, "Please, God!" But God would not listen to him, for he had been killing flies. This was what came of it. And he thought of those yellow blots with shame and hatred.

A large red hand was picking up the papers. The backs of the fingers were tufted with brown hair. Billy watched, fascinated. And then from still eyes, like a cornered animal, he stared into his father's wind-veined face. His own cheeks flushed. How absurd he must look!

"Come out of it! What are you doing there?"

Billy could not explain, but laid the ledger on the desk.

"I wasn't reading it," he said. "I promise."

He could have bitten his tongue out for this remark, and his neck burned. He felt his father's remote eyes looking down on him, and the glassy sneers of the deer-heads round the walls.

"You know I won't have you children making a bear-garden of the office!"

But the big man was suddenly embarrassed, feeling the gulf between himself and his son. And he made excuses. He was a busy man, without time to reach their immature minds. At any rate, one was enough. And he shrugged. His wife seemed to give up her whole time to them. But he was troubled by the thought of two locked doors facing one another at the end of a passageway.

"All right, old chap," he said, fumbling. "No trouble with the horses this morning? That's the boy. Game for tomorrow? Good."

And he nodded his head, winking, manly, buffeting Billy with restraint on the chest.

"All right, old chap. Run along now."

Billy ran along. His feet beat fiercely on the verandah. And, hearing them, his father sat perplexed. He shook his head. Must see more of the children. But what the devil was his son doing under the desk? He liked a boy to stand up for himself. And he squared his shoulders and opened the ledger.

"Billy!"

But Billy was chasing Janet through the orchard, stumbling over the furrows between the pink cherries and the clouded pears.

"I'll kill you!" he cried. "It was your fault. I'll murder you when I catch you."

And he ran panting, with a pain in his chest, fiercely forgetting, after long-legged Janet with her short flying skirt and bobbing hair, who slipped through the fence and was away like the wind over the green paddocks.

"You can't catch me," sang Janet, looking back through fair hair. And, "Ha ha!" she mocked from the graveyard. Then she was lost, swallowed up. And the great pines sighed.

"Ah!" said the black pines, leaning over. Brier-roots clutched the stone. Their tangled arms had torn the netting from the fence, and the gate hung loose on one hinge.

"Jan-et!"

Billy searched amongst the tombstones, peering here, peering there, through the bare briers in the shadow of the pines.

"Janet! Come out, I know you're here."

But he was alone.

"Come out, Jan. Where are you? I won't touch you. I give in. Promise."

Lost amongst the grave gravestones.

7

"Please, Jan."

And there she was, balancing, with one leg out and arms wide, on a leaning tombstone, smiling her secret smile. She stood still in sunlight on the stone, flushed from her run and victory, and daffodils were bright below her.

"What did he say?" she said.

"Not much." Billy turned away, diffident, indifferent.

"Go on, tell me, Billy."

"He didn't say anything." And Billy scowled.

"I'll bet he said, 'Keep out of the office!'" And Janet began to chant, "Keep out of the office! Keep out of the office!" till Billy, cheered, joined in.

"Well, old chap," he said in a deep voice. "Any trouble with the horses, old chap?"

Their pealing laughter rang through the graveyard. Billy strode, clop, clop.

"No trouble, eh? That's the chap."

"Oh!" Janet was giggling. "Oh!" merrily mocking. They were both happy with the intimacy of this secret between them. And, coming down from her tombstone, she walked with him arm-in-arm across the graves. The daffodils shook in the wind, and the hips of the briers danced, glinting.

"Here's old Wise's grave," said Janet, and she lifted a pincushion of moss from the rotting granite. "'The loving husband of Phillipa Sarah.' Philippa! Oh! Phillipa Sarah!"

The young heads touched beneath the pines, and their laughter was mingled.

"Silly old Wise," Janet said, and she stamped up and down the grave. Death, what was death on a fine morning? A fraud like Santa Claus. And she mocked the

8

pious faces and don'ts and hush, claiming a victory over that strange world of grown-ups where death had a meaning.

Billy stamped, too. And, to outdo his sister, who was only a girl, he had a good idea. The thin stream played on the tombstone. So much for old Wise. Happily the children straggled back through the sharp sunlight to the house for lunch.

III

Clamour!

The alarm clock was crowing in the children's sleep-out to the dark morning. Billy leapt from bed and was half dressed when his teeth began to chatter. He looked out fearfully through the wire gauze. The stars were high and pale, and the far pines stood darkly, like fists, against the coming light. A terrible dread ran its fingers up Billy's spine.

"I'm sorry, God. I'm sorry, truly, God."

Through the wall, he could hear his father's steady breathing.

"Jan, are you awake?"

A whisper, "Yes, Billy."

"It's terribly dark, isn't it? I wish ..."

And he sat down on Janet's bed. She could feel him shiver, and suddenly she clutched him to protect him, thrilling at the same time with the panicky joy of fear.

"Oh, Billy," she cried, half laughing, half awestruck, "there's something outside. Don't go, Billy!"

But, as Billy struggled with her, he forgot momentarily the thing outside and the remote lifting of his father's eyes. He was conscious only of a desperate need to break free.

9

I Want a Shilling Too

It was during the late summer of that year that Janet started keeping a money-box. The money-box was a warm red affair from a Christmas stocking, a letter-box with a slot in the side and a strip of sticking-plaster round the top where Janet had opened it with a tin-opener to see how much money she had.

"Two, four, six," she counted, skinning back the plaster and herding the silver coins into her hand, like her father counting sheep. "That makes six shillings in all. When I've saved a pound, I'm taking a ticket to Sydney to visit Bert at Coogee."

Carefully, she tossed the shillings up and down in her palm so that they glinted white in the sunlight, an exciting frosty glitter that made her eyes shine and her heart turn over inside her like a fish. Then she clattered the money back into its box and, in a tent of hair, thumbed on the plaster.

"But what about me?" Billy said. "I earn it too."

"Oh, you!" said Janet. "They wouldn't trust you. You haven't a head for business."

She was delighted with this remark, borrowed from their father, and had to hum a small song under her hair to keep herself from giggling; but it annoyed Billy.

"I have a head for business," he said. "You see. I

10

have a head for business too. And if you don't give me my share, I won't go away when they ask us. Then where will you be?"

"Now see what you've done," Janet said. "You've got my hair all caught up with the sticking-plaster."

But she did not seem really annoyed, and even rolled the shillings out again for Billy to hold for a minute. Holding them under his eye, each with its bearded king, and kangaroo and emu on the reverse propping up a shield, Billy was astonished once again at the ease with which they earned them. It didn't make sense. But there they were, and sliding them from one hand to the other he said, "Know what I'm going to do with mine? I'm going to buy a cattle-pup."

It was as easy as that. But Janet had started fidgeting.

"Don't throw them about like that," she said. "You'll lose them. Here, put them back."

And when they were safely gummed down again and the money-box was stowed away in the roots of the maybush and they were loitering back up the gravel path, Janet put her thin arm around Billy's shoulders and said, "We can't have a cattle-pup *and* a trip to Sydney. But I'll tell you what: I'll get Bert to send you back a fishing-line, or a surf flag, or even a bit of rope from the reel."

Billy, kicking stones, thought this over. What could he do with a surf flag? Perhaps he could set it up at the creek. Moodily, in self doubt, he kicked at the stones. Perhaps Janet was right and he didn't have a business head after all.

"Or Bert might even send you his photograph," Janet said.

11

Bert was Elsie's boyfriend. He was a lifesaver at Coogee, and was never out of a bathing costume except in the winter when he swept out a pub and threw people out the doors. He could do anything. And during the hot early afternoons the children lay about on the linoleum in Elsie's bedroom, their towels and costumes piled ready by the door, and listened to Elsie talking about Bert.

It was a corner room opening onto their sleep-out, and often Billy wandered off through the door, or leant far out one of the high vined windows, for a breath of fresh air; for Elsie's room smelt. It was a smell Billy always associated with housemaids, sweet and stale like pear-blossom; and somehow the thought of Bert always brought the same smell with him into his mind.

"Always fidgeting and fooling about," Elsie said, licking a curl into place in the glass. "What are you up to now? Letting in flies?"

Billy laughed his breath out among the vines and said, "Seeing where the ghost walks."

"Ghosts?" Elsie said. "Stuff and nonsense! Besides, they don't have feet."

"This one did. Emmy heard it, didn't she, Jan? Up and down a hundred to the dozen; and right under this window."

"More like old Sol with a bee in his pants!"

Elsie laughed with all her young body. Emmy! Well, who'd have thought it! Then, catching herself in the glass, she pared and refined until nothing was left but a half-smile like a paper flower between her teeth.

"And so la-di-da!" she mocked. "Kiss my foot! But you never can tell."

"You can laugh," Billy said, "but Emmy heard it."

"There's ears!"

"Getting back to Bert," Janet said, defending their old cook. "Does he really sweep out a pub?"

Somehow this did not fit in with the character of the lifesaver.

"Only in the winter." Elsie powdered, with pursed lips.

"But a pub? He sweeps out a pub, like a stable boy?"

"Maybe that's where he gets his smell," said Billy.

"What's all this about Bert smelling?"

Elsie's face was innocent with astonishment. Her man was in danger, crumbling away in these children's minds. And in panic she seized the paste photograph from her dressing-table.

"Smell!" she cried. "There he is, third from the right. You can't smell in the sea all day."

And indeed, Bert, third from the right, knee up, eyes to the front, marching in his costume across the white sands beneath the unfurled flag of his lifesaving club, did not look like a man who smelt. Billy wondered how the idea had ever come to him, and hoped it would never get back. He was for all the world like a smooth-running engine, the perfect hero. Engines only smelt when they got old.

"Imagine thinking that of Bert!" Elsie, hand to cheek, sat down on her stool, holding their impressed gaze. "Whoever put such a wicked thought into your heads? And as for sweeping out hotels"—for she needed to dig in—"someone's got to do it. You wouldn't like to arrive on holiday and find peanuts and orange-peel all over the foyer, would you?"

Even Janet conceded, "Hotels are different."

And Billy, quite excited, cried, "Does he sweep out Petty's, then?"

"Something like that."

"And throw the people out?"

"If they don't behave themselves."

"Wiss!"

Billy's uncles always stayed at Petty's. There were the uncles on his father's side, tall, hand-folding, shoulder-squaring men, always being called to long-distance telephones, who each had a formula for greeting Billy. His Uncle George, for instance, had once surprised him burning a snail with a magnifying glass. "Very interesting things, snails," Uncle George said. And now, whenever they met, it was, "Well, well, old chap? And how are the snails?"

Then there were his other uncles, seldom seen, mythical men who were always riding polo ponies up the front steps in his mother's stories, and dossing down on the billiard tables; and although Billy felt that they were more likely to be thrown out by Bert, he hoped very much it might be Uncle George.

"Show me how he does it?" he cried, wide-eyed.

"Oh, like this," said Elsie and she took him firmly by the collar and the seat of his pants. "Bert calls it the bum's rush."

And away wheeled Uncle George, all knees and elbows in a bum's rush, out through the open door to land a belly-flopper on Janet's bed.

"Hooray!" cried Billy into the pillow. His opinion of Bert had never stood so high.

But it was when Elsie took them to the creek, as she did each summer afternoon while their governess was on holiday, that Bert was really at his best.

The creek, cool with willows, slanted through sand at the foot of the hill; and the children, like a rabbiting-pack, raced off in front of Elsie and the basket, mocking and calling until they came to the thistle patch. There Elsie passed them while they picked their way angularly on bare toes; and by the time they reached the flat and the Chinaman's garden, the party was together, except for Babs, a tiny figure crying "wait for me!" among the thistles.

"I dropped my towel," Babs cried. "I dropped my towel and it's full of prickles."

"Take no notice," Janet said, foot over knee, picking. "She will take her shoes off. She only does it to attract attention."

But there was an agonizing wait before Babs caught up and her nose was blown and Elsie moved off again like a hen with chickens.

Oh, the pleasure of luke-warm water after the dust and the thistles! Clear as tea, it slid over the mica sand; and the children stood legs-apart in midstream watching their feet disappearing beneath them. Elsie settled down with her basket in the elbow of a willow-root.

"Come here, Babs," she called, "and I'll take your things off."

Billy was sent away by Janet behind the willow to change.

"Why must I always go?" Billy complained.

"Because you're a boy."

"But Babs doesn't even wear anything."

"There's not much to Babs," Janet said.

"But we bath together."

Janet's changeable modesty always seemed to work against him.

"That's different."

"There is much to me," Babs cried, bending her round golden body back in sunlight. "There is too!"

"Now then, Babs, don't be rude," said Janet, "or I won't have you in my team."

And for the next hour they marched and paraded and saved lives, Billy and Janet being Bert in turns, while Babs, between laughter and tears, played the corpse, dragged from the shallows at the end of a length of binder-twine.

"Am I dead this time," she asked anxiously, "or just full up with salt water?"

"Shut up," said Billy, on his knees, pumping. "You're unconscious anyway. Pull her tongue out, Bert; that'll quieten her. And they often swallow it."

"'Any sand, seaweed or other matter,'" droned Janet from Elsie's manual, "'must be removed from the mouth.'"

"Ow!" cried Babs.

"Other matter," said Billy.

Lazily Elsie watched them from the tree. The freckled sunlight splashed her body, burning holes through the thin cotton of her dress. Bert, Bert, Bert! The summer air was full of his name, and drowsily Elsie relaxed in the embrace of the willow-root that was his strong right arm.

Billy dated Bert's fall from favour from the day Mr. Blake appeared on horseback above the creek bank.

"Ah!" said Blake from the sky. "Having a picnic, I see."

The effect was immediate.

Elsie sprang scarlet from the arms of the willow like a startled lover; and Janet, who had ruled for that one day that bathing with nothing on was allowed, streaked for her towel and stood with it to her lips, screened from Blake while remaining naked to the rest of the world.

"It's all right," said Billy, sloshing upstream. "It's only Mr. Blake."

"Only!" hissed Janet. "It's all your fault, Billy. You're always wanting to take your clothes off; and you look disgusting."

But Mr. Blake was quite at ease, heeling his horse down the side bank and clattering through the water.

"Mind if I join you?" he said. "Couldn't eat my lunch. Like concrete."

Mr. Blake was the jackeroo. He had arrived a month ago under a cloud, following a telegram that read: Delayed. Expect Me Thursday's Train. Love, Blake.

"Love!" their father said. "Love! His expectations for the next half year are dagging wethers."

But Blake explained that some girl had sent the telegram, a friend of his sister; bought a pipe and a fast motor-bike, and looked about him.

Now, on the sand, mouth full of scone, he repeated, "Just like concrete! How that cook makes bread like that I don't know. It's her art."

"Oh ... Emmy," Elsie simpered, pouring tea. "She's

too busy fooling around with Sol to think about bread."

Billy stared hard at Elsie, for Emmy did not fool around with anyone, unless it were God. And Blake was up sharp on his elbow, staring too.

"No!" he said. "Not our Emmy? I don't believe it."

Elsie flushed, as well she might, but she managed airily, "Oh, you've got to keep your eyes open."

Mr. Blake's eyes were very wide open, gold as the eyes of a fox; and then they narrowed into laughter.

"Well, the old trout!" he said. "I thought she died years ago."

"Oh, you've got to get up early," Elsie said; "or late, in this case."

Billy noticed that Mr. Blake's laughter came out like the tea from the thermos: the sound started at his lips and then went deeper.

"Still a kick in the tail!" he cried. "Elsie, you're a discovery!"

He was still staring at Elsie, who was laughing too, her eyes running off merrily amongst the teacups and then returning, delighted with her lie.

"Elsie!" snapped Janet, coming fully clothed and haughty from behind the willow. "Watch the tea. You're pouring it all over the scones."

But Mr. Blake's laughter won the day, and soon they were all making fun of Emmy except Janet, and Elsie forgot to crook her little finger from the cup and kept offering their scones to Mr. Blake.

"Go on," she said. "They'll do you good."

Mr. Blake ate them and Elsie smiled. It was a strange broad smile for the world in general; but when it met Mr. Blake's she coloured up slowly, as if he had surprised her getting undressed.

"Well, well," said Blake, stretching and rising, "now I know where the good tucker is."

And he cantered off with the reins so tight that old Kismet reared and side-stepped like a two-year-old.

V

After that, Mr. Blake turned up by accident two or three afternoons a week. Elsie packed a larger basket and spent a longer time in front of her glass. So their descent of the hill was slower and Elsie's freshness lay deeper under powder. Also the children's games changed.

"Today," Mr. Blake said, "we're having a long-distance cross-country race. See that willow way off up there—no, no, the far one—well, that's the turning point. On your marks, get set—go!"

And he burst the paper bag that the scones had been in.

Billy ran hard and usually got back first to find Elsie and Mr. Blake side by side in the elbow of the willow and the last of the tea gone. They did not seem pleased with his win, either.

"I think I like Bert best," Billy told Elsie. "I think we should get back to lifesaving."

Mr. Blake had not arrived that day, and Elsie was fidgety.

"Yes," she said. "Bert was all right. Bert knew how to treat a girl."

But then she said something that Billy never forgot, because it was the last time he remembered her mentioning Bert.

"Yes," she said, "Bert was all right, but he wasn't

19

good enough for me. He told me so himself. A man should never say that to a girl, or she'll believe him."

Never, Billy vowed, would he ever say that to a girl, no matter how she made him feel undressed.

But it was Babs who struck first, and that was where the shillings came into it.

"I think," Babs said, "I'll stay and play sand-castles. It's too hot for running."

"But we've thought of a special race for you, Babs," Mr. Blake said. "See those sandpipers off there? All you have to do is run around them and home."

"I think I'll stay," Babs said, filling her bucket. "I like it here."

"But, Babs," Elsie said, "sandpipers are nice."

Babs up-ended her bucket and made a castle on the sand.

"Janet," Mr. Blake said, "I've decided to give a prize."

"How much?" said Janet.

"The prize is a shilling, but all contestants must take part in the race. There's no hurry home."

"First or last?"

"Last is the winner, but you get the prize."

"Come on, Babs," Janet said. "There's better sand for castles up the creek."

And Babs was led off screaming while, hand in hand, Blake and Elsie stood beneath the willow, watching them go.

VI

"But it isn't fair," Billy said. "I work just as hard as you do."

20

They were back to their old argument over the silver shillings—eight in all.

"Very well then, you go and tell him."

And carefully Janet drew the bucket away from the sand.

"Ah!"

"I'm sick of silly old sand-castles," Babs said, and razed it with her toe. "Let's all go back."

"But you haven't seen this one," said Janet, refilling the bucket.

"Well, I will go, see," said Billy. "You see if I don't." And he marched off down the creek between the high black-soil banks.

The day was hot, but Elsie and Mr. Blake were under the rug, right under, so that Billy really did not know what to do. There was nowhere to knock, so he splashed heavily through the water. The rug was still.

"Mr. Blake," he called, "I want a shilling too."

Silence. Perhaps they were asleep after all.

"I want a shilling," Billy chanted. "I want a shilling too."

"If you don't go away," came from the rug, "you'll get something you're not expecting."

It was then that Billy knew he had made a mistake, but for some reason he found that he was committed, he could not leave. It was like his dream. His feet stuck fast in the sand and he heard in anguish his silly high voice piping, "I want a shilling, I want a shilling, I want a shilling too."

Perhaps it was his head for business that kept him there, or the thought of Janet, but he remembered hating himself and that silly high voice; and when the record clicked on again and Mr. Blake caught him up and slapped his ear, he was glad. The ear stung like

21

bees and he smiled. It was what he deserved.

Soon after that, the weather changed and there was no more swimming for that year. And, though it was not his fault, Billy knew that Janet blamed him for it and the loss of her shillings. Elsie was off-hand too, and for some time Billy felt just as he did after lessons about the bad kings.

The good kings made him fine and brave; but after lessons about the bad kings, he asked himself if he would have done any better, and answered that he would not. And lying awake at night in their sleep-out, the possums scolding the moon outside, he saw quite clearly that he would end up like King John with the barons in charge, or like Bert, who was not even good enough for Elsie.

VII

It was perhaps because of this that he woke one night and heard the ghost walking outside Elsie's window. The door was closed, but he heard it quite clearly—the creak of feet on gravel. In one bound he was in Janet's bed.

"The ghost!" he whispered. "Listen!"

He could feel Janet listening with all her taut thin body, and, sure enough, there was the step again and the grate of the wire screen.

"It's getting into Elsie's room," said Billy. "We'd better warn her."

But to his astonishment, Janet said, "You wait here. I'll go."

She paused till all was quiet, and then, light as a ghost herself, while Billy shivered, she slipped to the door. The handle hardly groaned in turning. As silently the door shut behind her.

For an eternity, Billy lay sweating in the cold.

What was happening? What should the king do now?

In a trance of fear, he got out of bed and walked to the door. There Janet met him, coming back.

"It's all right," she whispered. "Come back to bed."

"But Elsie! What's happening to Elsie?"

"Come back to bed."

There, giggling, Janet pressed a warm two-shilling piece into his cold palm.

"It's for you," she said. "Elsie sent it."

And, in spite of the mystery, Billy slept soundly all that night, for he knew that he was forgiven.

I Wouldn't Miss
Christmas

I

Overhead in the still summer sky above the orange-tree, swallows were feeding their young on the wing, meeting and hanging breast-to-breast at the top of steep curves. Watching their windy flight over the creek and the yellow paddocks, Janet said:

"Wouldn't it be good to be grown up?"

She would dip, fly, over Bald Hill and the metal towns, mountains and pointed waves.

"But you'd miss Christmas," Billy said.

"They have Christmas, too."

"But they don't get much. A book or a pair of pliers."

"I wouldn't miss Christmas," Babs said.

"You'll miss it if you go on dragging your feet on Len's paths."

"You're doing it too."

Janet pointed her shoulders.

"I know," she said. "Let's play grown-ups. Let's dress up in their clothes."

For the children had the house and garden to themselves. Everyone else had gone to town to vote.

"That's a good idea," said Billy.

In the cool tall bedroom where they had been born, where their mother used to sit at night brushing her

24

long hair while they said their prayers, where their earliest memories moved like sun and shade in the vine-filtered light, Janet began taking out silks and treasures, enchanted in the scents of rosemary. The dim colours ran through her hands like water.

"I think ..." she said, fair head on one side, lips together. "How does this suit me?"

"What about me?"Babs said. "Who am I going to be?"

"Oh, you're too small. Nothing would fit you."

"I want to be mummy," Babs wailed.

"I'm mummy. We can't have two, stupid."

"I don't care, I want to be ..."

"I know ..." Janet's voice was suddenly affected, honeying over her impatience. "Keep quiet, and I'll dress you up. There"—the corners of her eyes were merry and white—"you can be Miss Frost."

"But she smells," Babs wailed.

"You're Miss Frost," Janet said, "or you don't play. But you can wear mummy's clothes. Billy, guess who Babs is."

"What's going on in here?"

Billy came thumping sternly out of their father's dressing-room in a pair of riding-boots that met his short pants above the knee. An old army tunic dwarfed him for a greatcoat, and their father's new city hat with the dents in it rocked on his ears. He had a boot-black moustache.

"What are you children up to now?"

Janet rolled among the silks, sprang up to adjust him.

"You almost frightened me," she said. "Just for a second. Here, I'll fix you. Say it again."

But Billy wrenched away, pacing stonily, struggling to retain his pose.

"Late as usual, Josephine."

But when he went to look at his watch, the sleeve of the tunic hung down and he ran laughing from the room. A moment later he was back.

"I'm sick of waiting," he said. "I'm sitting in the car."

Janet laughed more than ever.

"I want to play mummy," said Babs.

"You can't. You're Miss Frost."

"Come on," Janet said. "It'll be fun. You'll be funnier even than daddy."

In two minds, Babs gazed at her small figure in the dim glass.

"I expect," she said, "I could tuck some socks down my smock."

"Oh, yes!"

"But hurry up," Billy said.

The girls were ages getting dressed. Billy paced and fidgeted about the room, glancing at them, walking out and coming in again, no longer acting, while Janet smiled secretly, alone and bewitched in the feminine mirror-world of lace and powders.

"There," she said, dusting the rouge on her cheeks, "I really am quite like mummy."

"Oh, come on," Billy said. "Don't be all day. Really, Janet, you spoil everything."

"If you hurry me any more," Janet said, "I won't play."

Her eyes, as she looked at him from the looking-glass, were wide and candid. Billy turned and walked to the door. He stood there for some time, rattling the china doorknob.

"You're always late," he said. "You spoil everything."

"Button me up," said Babs.

But at last they were ready. Janet swept across the floor, her small fair head tilted upwards, while Babs trailed behind, a tiny pouter-pigeon, tripping on her skirts. In the unfamiliar sitting-room they all paused, self-conscious of a sudden, at a loss.

"The flowers," Janet said in a strained little voice. "They're lovely this year."

She began adjusting a vase with her long fingers. She really did not feel like playing. Billy's impatience had upset her. For some reason she had the feeling that their governess, the overseer, the jackeroos, were all in the room. The men had risen and were looking at her.

Billy, hiding laughter, paced to the fireplace. Hands behind his back, swaying from heels to toes, he glanced about the room. He was enjoying himself, his irritability forgotten.

"Well, my dear. Children all right?"

"Oh, yes. Thank you."

"That's good. Garden looks well."

"Yes it does, doesn't it?"

Billy was really doing marvellously. He was glancing about, at ease, making the conversation, just like their father in his rare boisterous moods before dinner. But Janet still felt constrained, shut in, as if the room were full of strangers. Even Billy seemed different; he had spoiled the day.

The chintz curtains stirred, and, gazing out at the blond wavering paddocks, he had a good idea.

"The water," he said. "The pump has broken down. You'll have to go steady on the watering."

Immediately Babs broke into tears. Her eyes closed and her mouth opened.

"The flowers," she wailed. "They'll all die. What will mummy say?"

Billy, standing at the fireplace in his big boots, looked at her in amazement. He thought he had been doing very well. But Janet gave him a swift look and led Babs crying into the bedroom.

"There," she said, "it was only a game. There's still plenty of water."

"I must have been really good this time," Billy said from the door. "She thought it was real. I can do it when you don't laugh ... What's the matter, Jan? Aren't we going to play any more? Oh, come on!"

Janet was undressing Babs, folding the things away in the sweet-smelling drawers, doing everything the way their mother did.

"Come on, Jan. I don't understand."

He hovered about the room, annoyed, bewildered, feeling like crying himself, clumsy in his big clothes.

"We'd only just started. I don't understand," he kept saying.

"That's just the whole trouble," Janet said.

But suddenly she was sorry for him—for her father as well as her mother.

"Oh, well," she said. "You get changed and we'll all walk down the avenue and meet mum and dad at the first gate."

Outside the swallows were still swinging and feeding in the vast cloudless sky.

The Archway

I

When their mother spoke about *men*, the children had visions of grave, bearded, courteous giants who sat at the tops of tables like their grandfather and stood up when ladies came into the room and gave considered opinions over whiskies at their clubs. But sometimes these giants relaxed, and then they tossed for sovereigns on the top step of Petty's Hotel and galloped tandem-pairs over five-bar gates; and if money was needed for a good cause, they auctioned their hats for one hundred and fifty guineas in the foyer of the Hotel Australia.

"Well, that is what *men* have told me," she would say, opening her brown eyes; and that was the end of the argument.

Mr. Marshall, the overseer, was a man.

Mr. Marshall had curly brown hair that the children liked to pull when he sat in the sun under the elm-trees on Sunday. The muscle of his right arm was so strong that it would burst his coat if he put it up to show them; and he came from the north-west plains where their grandfather lived.

"Tell us how you tripped the emu," Janet said, sidling onto his lap.

"Yes," said Billy, flopping down on top of her.

"I want to sit on his knee too," Babs wailed.

"Now then, children," Mrs. Dalrymple said. "Leave Mr. Marshall alone."

And her eyes met Marshall's in a smile of sympathy, for Mrs. Dalrymple loved her children, and Marshall was a little in love with her.

"Mr. Marshall," Miss Frost said, "I wonder if you would help me get this nail out of my shoe?"

Their governess always seemed to be having trouble with her clothing when the children played with the overseer.

II

It was nearing the end of winter, and each evening before their bath the children ran up the frost-hardened road to the stables to meet Mr. Marshall coming home from the lambing paddocks. Usually on the way they met their father striding in thought between the darkening elms.

"Well," he said, "Well, what have you three been up to today?"

"Oh, just mucking about," Janet said, dragging her foot behind her on the gravel.

And their father laughed or made some joke; and sometimes he lifted one finger and caught it in the palm of his other hand and said, "Come on now, you must have done something. Tell me one thing, one thing", catching and releasing the finger while the children stood dumb, running back through their minds and finding the day a blank behind them.

"Did you go riding?"

"Oh, yes," Billy said, stepping forward with relief. "Yes, we went riding to Spring Creek. And—and we saw a fox."

"Well, there you are, then"—rumpling Bab's hair with his hand. "That's better than 'mucking about', isn't it?"

And while the children raced each other up the hard red road he continued down the road. The verandah boards rang, the gauze door banged; and at the sideboard Doctor Dalrymple unlocked the decanter and took out one of the thin silver-necked bottles. Glass at arm's length, he poured out one inch—the daily measure—added soda, and, with feet apart, he drained his whisky at a draught.

"They saw a fox," he said, wiping his greying moustache.

And for some reason he hesitated a moment before relocking the decanter and striding off to his dressing-room to change.

III

At dinner their father sat at the head of the table and their mother at the other end said grace. Miss Frost bowed her head and kept her eyes sideways on the children; Janet looked under her brows at Billy; Mr. Blake, the jackeroo, looked embarrassed; Mr. Marshall smiled down at his brown hands. Then they all lifted their heads and whisked their table-napkins out of their rings and their father ground knife on steel.

"Ah!" he said. "I see we've got bird again. No trouble in the fowlyard, I hope?"

He looked serenely over his reading-glasses down the long table at his wife.

Miss Frost gave a little shriek of delight and horror, and Billy said, "Foxes!"

This was his table trick—the short, well-timed, humorous aside of no more than six words, or there he was in the silence. It never failed to please his father, who glanced at him with momentary interest while he laughed.

"Well, well," he said, looking up through his glasses, "I thought there must be something more to that fox you saw. Very good!"

But their mother had flushed a little and was explaining: some of the fowls were moulting; she was weeding out the ones that didn't lay. Doctor Dalrymple only laughed the more, and, rising, he pinioned a ruddy chicken with the twin prongs of the fork.

"There's only one way to carve a bird," he said. "The secret is, never move the fork!"

Dexterously he dismembered the fowls and laid back the creamy shavers of breast. It was like the dismantling of a machine or the perfect analysis of a problem. While he carved, no one spoke. The yellow-box log cracked in the open hearth, a possum whispered from the roof, Elsie carried round the plates, her chin wobbling at each step.

"Drumstick for you, Billy?"

It was a Sunday joke, and Billy laughed, though he always got the drumstick.

"Please don't wait," their mother said, smiling and sitting forward. "It will only get cold."

Janet put a hot potato in her mouth, turned very red and cough-coughed, turning her head to one side, swallowing it. Mr. Marshall slapped her back, feeling the delicate bone beneath his hand.

"You should have put it out, dear," their mother said.

32

"Too late now, I've swallowed it. I can still feel it though—just about here."

She smiled round the table through tears, her face still burning, and reached for the water.

"Like a little coal."

And Billy laughed.

"Always put it out." Their mother's smile was troubled. "It could be very bad for you."

"Never be afraid to spit it out," their father said. "You've got a very good precedent in Dr. Johnson. He was dining, I think, at Mrs. Thrale's. Only time he was ever caught out, to my knowledge."

Doctor Dalrymple had taken off his glasses and was glancing down both sides of the table, rounding up attention. Billy rolled his bread-pills under his plate; Mr. Blake paused, his fork half-way; Miss Frost blinked into a bright smile and put her grey head on one side for listening.

"Yes—at Mrs. Thrale's. He was dining in very good company when the same thing as happened to you, Janet, happened to him. He put a hot potato in his mouth. But, unlike Janet here, the great man spat it back, and glancing round the table"—Doctor Dalrymple lifted his own spiked brows and gazed imperiously down his nose—"glancing round the table he said, 'A fool, sir, would have swallowed that!'"

Miss Frost began to titter.

"Hold on, hold on! .. 'A fool' said Johnson, 'would have swallowed that!' But someone on his left, I forget who—one of the lesser guests—caught him out beautifully. 'Ah, but then, Doctor,' he said, 'a wise man wouldn't have put it in in the first place!' Completely stumped him! You can imagine ..." Dalrymple's wind-veined face had crimsoned with delight and he sat

33

forward; but Janet had flushed too.

"I'm not," she said.

Her long lashes were down and her pouting lips trembled.

Their father was taken aback. The laughter in his eyes greyed to steel and he lifted his head.

"Not what?"

"I'm not a fool!" Janet shouted, and burst into tears.

There was a moment's silence. Then Mr. Marshall's handkerchief was out and Janet was blowing into it and their mother had reached out and was soothing her hand.

"Your father was talking about Dr. Johnson, darling; not about you at all."

"Leave me alone," Janet whispered, catching jagged breaths. "I'll be all right in a minute."

"Really, Josephine," their father said, "Janet will have to have early tea with Babs if she can't behave better than this. To take up a thing like that—a story about Johnson. Only by the widest stretch—"

"I'll speak to her afterwards," Miss Frost said through straight lips.

Janet lifted raw eyes.

"Dinner is a time for good talk," their father was proceeding. "Goodness knows it's hard enough to lift the conversation above sheep and flies. I keep my end up. Sometimes I think I talk too much, and quite purposely I say nothing. What happens? There is a silence."

He paused. Down by the creek a curlew cried.

"When I was young my father sat at the head of the table—brurrh!"

Doctor Dalrymple put a fist at each side of his plate,

34

hollowed his back, thrust out his lips and glared through twinkling eyes.

"There we were, five girls and four boys, and your grandmother in a lace collar at the far end. That was before the big drought, of course."

And suddenly his eyes softened, seeing it all as he knew it as a child, but with new knowledge—before the dry years that broke his father. The curlew haunted the darkness.

"A fine man," he said. "A fine man! Yes, as I was saying, there he was, head of his own table. And it was, 'And what do you think, Richard?', 'And what is your opinion of that, Joan?' Oh, very different indeed from these days! You spoke when you were spoken to. 'Little boys,' he would say, 'should be seen and not heard.'"

"Like the Queen and the salad," said Billy.

Doctor Dalrymple checked; he laughed; he threw back his head. Tears of laughter came into his eyes.

"Oh, very good! I told you that, did I? About the Queen and the salad? Very skilfully timed. Real wit!"

And he took out his glasses and looked over them at Billy, smiling and curious, puzzled by this shy boy of his, these momentary glimpses of a mind.

"I told you that, did I?"

And he went on to retell the story of Queen Victoria eating the slug after silencing the prince.

"Yes," he said, "perhaps things are better nowadays. Let the young have their heads. You picked me up very well."

Billy, having said seven words for the meat, smiled modestly at his plate while glory burned his ears. Janet kicked him under the table. It was only then they became aware that their mother was talking to Mr. Marshall.

She was leaning sideways towards him, nodding and smiling as if at a dinner party, and, when she listened, her fair face lit up expectantly, or a dreaming, brooding mood narrowed her wide eyes.

"Yes," she said, "after the ball they all came home in four-in-hands. There were I can't tell you how many in the house! We had to set up card-tables in the dining-room. You remember Jim Allenson?"

"Yes," Marshall said, suddenly conscious of the heat of the fire. "We're talking of the Goolah Picnics, Doctor."

"Yes, yes," their father said. "We're out of the way here. A dull district. Golf with Grant on Sundays." He sighed, long-sighted eyes lost with the curlews by the creek. "It was different in the mess during the war ... men from all walks of life ... Well"—his hands were on the arms of his chair—"are we ready, my dear?"

Mrs. Dalrymple rose. There was a grinding of chairs.

IV

After dinner the children always changed into pyjamas before going into the sitting-room to say good night. In slippers and belted dressing-gowns they slithered to the door; there were scuffles and broken whispers; demurely they filed through the tall room with its chintz coverings and burning hearth.

Their father sat in his leather chair, a coffee cup on his knee, an open book on his lap, talking politics or pastures with Mr. Marshall. Miss Frost stitched, her eyes on the children; their mother dreamed over her embroidery; Mr. Blake yawned at the fire.

"Good night, dad."

Janet kissed his forehead; Billy shook his hand.

"That's the boy."

A wink and a nod.

Then they hugged their mother.

"Don't forget to say your prayers, darlings."

And passing Mr. Marshall's chair Janet flicked his knee with the tips of her long fingers, blue eyes to the side, merry and proud, and said, as light as you like, "Good night!"

"Janet"—Miss Frost had stopped stitching—"Ladies do not act like that in front of gentlemen."

"Her!" Janet said, climbing in between frosty sheets in their sleep-out. "What does she know about it, anyway? She isn't even married."

"I wonder ..." Billy said. He was hollowing a warm hole in the pillow for his head. "I wonder what they do now, Jan?"

"I know what Mr. Blake does."

The children giggled, feeling their beds warming and closing around them.

In the sitting-room the golden log broke; the scattered coals darkened.

"Well, to the office." Doctor Dalrymple rose.

His steps rang on the verandah; his voice echoed from the telephone. "That you, Dick?" Through the thick plaster wall they heard the snapping of a typewriter, the minute tinkle of its bell. Mr. Blake yawned again at the fire and looked at his watch, noticing the fine hairs on his wrist.

"Time to turn in," he said. "Early to bed and early to rise."

He looked down at Marshall with subtle composure. "Good night."

But as the light closed behind him his heart was

beating. Would she be there? He was meeting Elsie, the housemaid, behind the woodheap at nine. On silent soles he felt his way down the dark passageway and let the side wire door close behind him on his hand. Ten thousand stars shot their arrows through the night.

Marshall rose restlessly, stretched, and smiled quietly down at lifted toes, his back to the fire.

"What are you making?" he said.

"Oh, this is only the children's mending." Miss Frost shrugged.

"It's a little mat," Mrs. Dalrymple said, "to stand the flowers on, on the piano."

She held it up, smiling. For no reason, this was the happiest time of her day. Her work was over; the children were in bed. She could knit and muse and talk to these two friends. It was a fortune that they got on so well together.

"Now, the flowers you've got there now," Marshall was saying, nodding towards the piano. "Wouldn't they be narcissus polyanthus?"

He had put his hands in his pockets and closed them, parading his knowledge. Really, sometimes he reminded Mrs. Dalrymple of her son.

"Nearly," she said. "They're narcissus poeticus. The first of the year. It's spring."

And laying her embroidery in her lap, she smiled across to the other woman.

"Would you believe it, Frosty? I took him round the garden last Sunday and he knew the Latin names of—oh, well, quite a number anyway—of the plants and shrubs. Though sometimes"—and she laughed—"he mistook them for very rare species. I didn't know before you were so fond of gardening."

Miss Frost bit off a thread.

"Humph," she said, knotting. "So that's what that book was about that came through the post a week or two back!" Mrs. Dalrymple paused. She laughed.

"Oh, you're too caustic, Frosty."

And she took up her embroidery again.

Yes, Frosty was caustic. Mrs. Dalrymple expected it was because she had not married. Marriage mellowed a woman, she thought; at least that was what people said. Perhaps it was not too late yet.

She glanced up a moment, meditating. Miss Frost was grey—at least ten years older than herself; but her figure was still very good. There was no chance for her here. Perhaps she might ask someone down? A row of tiring bachelors swept off their hats in her mind. So many thinning crowns!

But Mrs. Dalrymple could not keep her thoughts on them; she could not stop the little smile at her lips.

Perhaps Mr. Marshall had cheated; but didn't that make it all the more charming? He had done it for her.

Mrs. Dalrymple began to hum a little, to croon over the coloured threads in her lap.

There was no harm in it. And it was a delight to share with someone her passion for flowers. Dreamily she re-entered the Sunday garden while cocks crowed and the little beaks of the daffodils showed their first yellow. Very soon the whole orchard would be in bloom.

"A penny for your thoughts," Marshall said.

Mrs. Dalrymple was quite confused.

"I'm worried about the Doctor," Miss Frost said. "It's so bleak and cold in that office next door—and lonely."

"Yes, I often tell him. He should do his work in the daytime. But it is his way; and that's that."

"In the daytime," Miss Frost said, "he is out in the

39

paddocks. The office work must be done some time—I expect."

"It is extraordinary," Marshall said. "He is planning. You'd hardly think you could judge to ten minutes just how much work twelve men can do in a day. Yet there it is every morning, typed out: the day's work; an exact day."

"There you are then," Miss Frost said, settling back and stitching.

"I don't see what more I can do." Mrs. Dalrymple was nettled, forced somehow to defend herself, a little hurt by the tone. "There's a fire; and I do my best to make the room comfortable. But, as you know, the Doctor likes his things left alone."

"It's the loneliness I'm thinking of."

"Frosty, now you're being absurd."

"Perhaps I am."

And she went on stitching at Billy's trousers, quick angular stitches, a button between the tight lines of her lips.

"What do you suggest? Shall we all go and sit in there? He *would* be pleased!"

"I'm sorry I brought the subject up."

Miss Frost fumbled in the valley of her high chest and brought out the handkerchief Mrs. Dalrymple had given her for Christmas. She blew her nose, sniffing.

"I was only thinking of the Doctor, I'm sure. And then one is misunderstood."

Really for all her brusqueness, Miss Frost was a wet fish inside.

"I'd do anything in the world for the Doctor," Mrs. Dalrymple said. "Seriously, Frosty, what do you suggest?"

"I don't know, I'm sure. A door could be put

through to the office from this room; or, alternatively, an arch.''

Her nose was now red, and she blink-blinked at the blurred wall. To appease her became suddenly more urgent than the Doctor's loneliness. Mrs. Dalrymple gathered up her embroidery and stood facing the wall.

"An arch," she thought out aloud. "Bring one room into the other. It would not be unattractive. But then"—and she dropped her hand from her lip—"of course, my husband wouldn't hear of it."

Then the governess said a curious thing.

"You don't know what you can do till you try," she said. "Oh, dear! My handkerchief is all moist. I shouldn't be such an old water-cart."

V

"What is an archway, mummy?"

"Sssssssss!" hissed Janet and Billy.

It was a still late-winter morning. A solid square of sunlight blocked in the verandah; the leaves of the distant gum trees ran like water; orchard trees spiked the numb haze, and turf smoked in their frosted shadows.

"An archway?" their mother said, pouring morning tea. "Why, that's an archway there, Babs, with the grapes over it. What a funny thing to ask! Billy, take this cup to your father."

"Serves you right," Billy hissed, passing.

Babs never could keep a secret.

"I don't see," Babs said. "What would they want one for in the sitting-room?"

"Thanks, old chap."

"Sssssssss!"

41

"I won't sssssssss," Babs said. "See! I can talk if I want to. It sounds silly."

"Babs, what *are* you talking about?"

"They won't let me say a thing!" Babs wailed. "Miss Frost told us. They're putting up a silly old archway in the sitting-room."

Billy and Janet looked at one another. Miss Frost sipped tea with crooked fingers. Their father rustled his paper, cross-legged in the sun, hat tilted.

"They're always teasing me!"

"Billy!" Their father laid down his paper. "Are you teasing Babs again?"

"I only said about the silly old arch." Babs was sure of support from her father. "And they look at me like ... like ..."

She stood there in bloomers and sweater, minute and ruddy, and threw back her head and howled.

"There, there, there."

"Let's get to the bottom of this," their father said. "There's too much teasing in this family."

"They're mad. Who wants an arch in the sitting-room?"

"What is all this, Josephine?"

"It seems," their mother said, drying Babs's eyes— "blow! Now the other side—it seems that Babs has heard about a door, or an arch, rather, that I was discussing with Miss Frost, between the sitting-room and your office."

She looked over at the governess, who was helping herself to a finger of toast.

"An arch! Into my office? Never heard of such a thing!"

"I was going to mention it to you—at an opportune time. I thought you wouldn't like it."

"An arch! I should damn well think not! Has everyone here taken leave of their senses?"

"There is no need to shout, Andrew—there you are, Babs, you're tidied up again—we'll drop the subject."

"*Shout!*"

Doctor Dalrymple stopped shouting. He put on his glasses and looked over them at his wife. His voice became smooth, bantering. Women were children, after all.

"And who is shouting? Ah! A door—or an archway, rather—into my office. Very good. Why not two archways? Or a row of columns? And who was the—ah—architect of this plan?"

"I think it would be nice," Mrs. Dalrymple said simply. She glanced again at Miss Frost; then, meeting her husband's eyes, she drew an archway in the air with her hands. "It would bring one room into the other."

"Bring the sitting-room into my office? Or perhaps you mean my office into the sitting-room! And where do you suppose the work of the property is to be done?"

"I was only thinking of you, Andrew." Mrs. Dalrymple's voice was level, but the colour had died in her cheeks and the tea spilled as she put down her cup. "It is too cold and lonely in that room every night."

"Lonely! Lonely! Now, let us understand this, Josephine, once and for all ..."

Miss Frost rose silently. Silently she herded the children before her down the verandah. As the door closed they heard "... work to do without pulling the house down" and their mother's stubborn "I am very keen on the idea."

"There you are, Babs," Billy said. "Now see what you've done!"

43

"Don't speak to her," Janet said.

"Children! You must learn to be more charitable. She is only a little girl."

Their mother did not come in for lunch. She was working in the garden.

VI

"I will not ..." Mrs. Dalrymple drove the fork into the rich brown tacky loam. "I will not"—laying over a sod—"have him speak to me like that!" The sod burst under the silver prongs. Worms, coloured like veins, moved blindly in the sunlight. The magpie stepped closer, beat one against a stake. "He has never done it before—in front of the children."

She paused and pushed back brown hair from her damp forehead. The mild wind chilled her face.

"Oh."

The governess was coming down the path with a mug of soup and biscuits on a tray.

"Thank you," Mrs. Dalrymple said. "I'm not hungry. I just forget time when I'm gardening."

Miss Frost was hurt. She stood looking at the magpie.

"It was not my place to say anything. Babs *will* chatter."

Mrs. Dalrymple took the soup.

"I made them promise," Miss Frost said. "Oh, I'm just a silly old fool!"

She took out the Christmas handkerchief. Mrs. Dalrymple took a biscuit.

"I don't know why I'm alive."

Mrs. Dalrymple drank the soup. It was hot,

44

delicious. It comforted. She bit the biscuit.

"Oh, Frosty," she said, "I don't know what I'd do without you."

"I can't understand the Doctor." Frosty snivelled. "It was so unlike him ... As if you weren't mistress in your own home!"

She raised her eyes. Mrs. Dalrymple replaced the empty cup.

"Thank you," she said. "That will do."

She was not going to discuss her private affairs with the governess.

But the peace of the garden was gone. She toiled on until late afternoon, turning and breaking the sods, her strong brown arms smeared with soil and sweat, her brown hair falling now and then over her eyes. Early mists crept up from the creek, chilling her. The cock-crows sharpened. She would have to go in.

But her gaze lingered like the light in the garden as she turned towards the house of which she was no longer mistress.

VII

Usually their mother's smile was like amber; you imagined you could see the centre of it right down inside her. But the next morning it was just a tightening of her curved lips; and her brown eyes were restless. The children began to fight with one another.

"Billy," Janet said, "I won't play with you if you cheat."

"I'm not cheating. You don't like being beaten, that's all."

They were playing table-croquet on the front verandah. A thin wind bared the white sticks of the gum-trees.

"You did."

"I didn't."

Janet laid down her mallet.

"I won't play with you," she said. "I won't play with you ever again."

"I don't care."

"I won't play with you at anything. I'll never play with you. Babs will be my friend."

"I won't play with you either."

Janet put her arm round Babs's head.

"We're girls, aren't we, Babs? We won't play with him, will we? Then you'll see."

"Who'd be a girl, anyway?"

"There's only one of you," Janet said. "Just think: all your life and never ever anyone to play with."

"When I grow up," Billy said uncertainly, "I'll go droving; and, and—drive four-in-hands over gates."

"They don't have them now; they have cars—see! You would look silly—and all on your own."

Janet pirouetted in the sun.

"Come on, Babs," she said, "let's go and play dolls. We'll leave him."

"Oho!" Babs said, taking her hand. "Can I hold Yvonne? We don't like boys."

Left alone, Billy played the coloured balls around the table. There was nothing—absolutely nothing—to do. He dragged the sleeve of his jersey along his nose. A lonely desert tract stretched out before him, the skyline broken by vast croquet-hoops. His mother kept coming out of the sewing-room and looking up the front path towards the stables.

"Billy, has your father gone out to the paddocks yet?

46

Go and see."

"In a minute."

Janet and Babs were coming along the side verandah past the pot-plants with a pram and an armful of dolls. They settled in the sun by a verandah-post, propping up the dolls and laying out tin tea-things. Billy became absorbed in his game.

"Whissss!" he whistled to himself. "Through two hoops at the one time!"

"Which do you like the best, Babs?" Janet was holding up two party frocks. "The pink or the blue?" Her fair hair hung down to one side as she considered. "Pink, don't you think? They're all girls."

"We're not listening to *him*," Babs said.

"Billy!" Their mother stood in the doorway of the sewing-room. "How many times have I got to tell you? Does no one listen to me any more?"

"It's always me!" Billy's lips went down, he turned his jaw, round tears squeezed out between the lashes. "They're all against me."

And with his face to the side, he ducked over the lawn, between the mandarins, to skulk and mope under the may-bush. Janet watched him, smiling.

"I don't know what's got into you children this morning," their mother said. "Just when I'm worried and upset myself."

She walked with quick agitated steps up the path towards the blacksmith's shop and the stables. Babs's eyes closed, her bottom-lip went forward.

"Shush," Janet said. "There, don't cry. Look, I'll give you Yvonne—all to yourself!"

47

VIII

When Billy came back, kicking pebbles up the gravel path, he found his mother, the girls, and Sol Jones in the sitting-room.

Sol Jones did the blacksmithing and carpentering about the place. He had black hair and warts on his nose and blackheads on his neck like frogs' eggs in the dam. His waistcoat hung open and his grey-striped working trousers were hitched to police-braces with nails. But in the blacksmith's shop on wet days, he was like some dark king, beating gold shoes in the blue light of the forge and tossing them to sigh in a Laurel tin while he talked gently to the tethered horses. Somehow, though, he looked out of place in the sitting-room.

Their mother was explaining about the arch, carving half-circles with her hands, while Sol nodded, a mattock over his shoulder.

"You see, it's quite simple, Sol. Just a matter of knocking the wall in. In fact, quite a small hole would do for the time being."

"I get yer, all right," Sol said, "as the saying is, Mrs. Dalrymple. You want a big sorter doorway—a harch, like." He fumbled in the pocket of his loose waistcoat. "There you are now. I've gone and left the makings in the shop! There wouldn't be a smoke in the house, by any chance, would there, Mrs. Dalrymple?"

"Why, of course, Sol. I'm so sorry."

Their mother hurried out as if she had neglected a favourite visitor.

"This harch, now," Sol said. "We're mates, ain't we? Yer mum seems terrible steamed up, terrible steamed up over something. The dad would know all about this harch, now, wouldn't he?"—jerking his charcoal head towards the wall.

But Janet had set her lips and shaken her head at Babs.

"Ah!" breathed Sol. "Yes, I was just saying to the kids here, Mrs. Dalrymple, that seems a terrible nice sorter wall to be knocking a hole in ... Thank you, I'm sure. It's not every day yer get a tailor-made, if you catch me."

"Well, Sol, you know what's to be done."

"Here," Sol said, stepping after her. "Just a shake, Mrs. Dalrymple. Them joists, now. Might bring the whole house down over our ears."

"Don't be silly, Sol. Those walls are two foot through."

"Two foot? Now, would they be that now? Two foot! H'm. Then there's not much use titivating 'em with the mattock, then. That's a certain." And he sighed. "Tell you what, now. I'd best talk this over with the boss. Two foot!"

"Sol," their mother said, "are you going to knock a hole in that wall or aren't you?"

"Now, if you put it to me like that now, Mrs. Dalrymple ..." Sol was fumbling in the other pocket of his waistcoat. "Wouldn't be a light in the house anywhere, would there? Seems I've left the matches too."

"Give me that pickaxe!" their mother cried. "Men! They call themselves *men*!"

And seizing the mattock in her sinewy brown hands, she swung it behind her head. A split ran up the wall-paper. Plaster fell. Three times she struck before, pale and straight, she handed the mattock back to Sol.

"There," she said. "Carry on."

"Well now." Sol gazed in admiration at this wild young wife the boss had taken. "Well now, Mrs. Dalrymple, that makes all the difference. How big would you be wanting this hole?"

But she had walked quickly out of the room.

"Lend us a hand now, Billy!" Sol cried. "I'll be wanting some trestles."

"Sssssss!"

Janet caught Billy's arm.

The curtain over Miss Frost's door stirred. A latch clicked.

"She was listening!"

IX

That night there was an angel passing.

The Doctor saw the hole as he squared his feet to drink his whisky. Luckily the decanter was at hand. He broke the rule of several years and felt better. Conversation that night was about women in history and the consequences. The children went to bed hushed. Nothing was said about the hole.

The trestles stood against the wall of the sitting-room; the plaster lay where it had fallen; the snapping of the typewriter and the ringing of its warning bell sounded clearly through the gap. But otherwise it was as if it had never been. This went on for five days. On the sixth the Doctor began to move his files to a room in the old part of the house. On the seventh he left for Sydney to attend a B.M.A. dinner.

The angel had passed.

"I don't know what it is," Mrs. Dalrymple said, turning to find Marshall beside her in the garden after Sun-

50

day lunch. "Spring seems to have hidden away this year. And then suddenly it is like an explosion." She paused, head on one side, as if listening. "You can almost hear it."

Down in the valley, the pallid cuckoo laid his notes.

"Now that there," Marshall said, pointing his toe, seeking a concrete image for his feelings. "Wouldn't that be ...?" He scratched his curly head.

"Ah," said Mrs. Dalrymple with a little smile. "That you would not know. It is not mentioned in Thwaites."

X

"That you, children?"

The children, stirring in their sleep-out, looked at one another.

"Yes, dad," Janet said.

It was the first they knew of their father's return.

"Well, well! ... Haven't you got a kiss for your poor old father?"

In a moment pyjama'd figures were clambering over the sill into the shadowy bedroom.

"Don't forget your dressing-gowns," from their mother. But it was too late. They were already bouncing onto the wide brass-knobbed bedstead where they all had been born.

Their father was lying back with his teeth out, his moustache raised in a smile, the abrupt line of his collar showing at his open neck.

"*That's* the kids! *That's* the kids!"

Janet covered him with kisses. Billy, wondering whether to shake hands, was pulled down too. Babs rode ride-a-cock-horse on his blanketed toe. Their mother lay beside him, smiling and rested, the plaits of her brown hair out on the pillow like a girl's.

"Well now, well now," when the first excitement was over. "Billy, go to that cupboard there and bring me—ahrum—there's something there."

And Janet's eyes were plates as he brought out a new cowtail stockwhip.

"Whizzz!"

He ducked for the door, remembered, kissed his father; and the next second the fall stung, echoing in the frost.

"Billy! You'll catch cold."

"I got myself a good one," he said, returning, showing the red weal.

In the second cupboard was a brass sewing-machine for Janet, and more abandoned kisses while Babs spied through the crack of the third.

"It really works," Janet said.

"Andy, you've been marvellous."

"Chose 'em all myself," their father said, smiling. "Took the whole morning. Now Babs: yes, that's right."

The little girl turned crestfallen from the open cupboard, a thin-spouted watering-can in her hand. She looked at it, she looked up, her lip trembled.

"Is this all?" she said.

"Darling, how marvellous!" called their mother, while Janet and Billy pulled faces and scowled. "Now you'll be able to help me water the garden."

"Would you like something else, Babs?"

"Yes," she said over her lip.

And this fabulous new father clambered long-legged out of bed and came back from his dressing-room with a bar of chocolate. Babs took it and smiled. For once there was no mention of not eating before breakfast.

"Usually," their father said, lying back with his family around him, "usually I don't bring presents. I like to be welcomed for my own sake. But since I've broken the rule ... Janet, is there anyone we've forgotten?"

"Ah!"

"Yes, Josephine," he said seriously. "I saw Braddocks on the way in. He'll have men out in a day or two to put that arch through and plaster the other room."

The ring was complete.

"Yes," he said later. "After thinking it over—I like the idea. It'll be somewhere to sit at night."

"These men ..." Mrs. Dalrymple's voice was tentative, for she knew her husband's moods. "You say they'll be out in a day or two?"

"Women!" The Doctor laughed. "Women! They go on as if life will be over at any minute!"

XI

And, indeed, life was very different for five or six days. The table talk swaggered; Mr. Blake was drawn out and found to have wit; their father's face glowed like the hearth; and the arch went through.

Miss Frost was a treasure at this time, sitting into the still of night stitching curtains, pins and thread sprouting like hairs from her thin lips. The late hours are the hours of intimacy, and the two women bent over the ash of coals, would meet each other's glance with the smile of conspirators.

"No, no, Frosty. I give you all the credit."

On the opening night there was wine for dinner—crusted bottles, borne lovingly from the box-room, that burnt in the mind like dusty jewels—and the children were allowed to stay up late in pyjamas and dressing-gowns. The pianola had been moved into the new bright room with its sweeping arch and striped curtains, and they all stood round it, their father singing in a sad old-fashioned voice, their mother's notes climbing, and the governess and overseer high and low behind. Only Mr. Blake excused himself; he left before nine to write some urgent letters for the morning mail.

"*O wert thou in the cold blast, on yonder lea, on yonder lea* ..."

Their father, pedalling, took their mother's hand, his eyes away with the curlews, remembering his own Scottish mother and the alien drought outside. Miss Frost's head settled a moment against Mr. Marshall's arm.

"Oh, I'm so sorry! I must have dropped off to sleep."

"Yes," said their mother. "It's late. The children are tired."

Babs was curled up on a cushion, pink hand open and spread.

"Ups-a-daisy!"

The two women looked down at the sleeping heads in the sleep-out. A kiss and tiptoe out.

"Yes," said Mrs. Dalrymple in the hall. "It was a great success. Thank you."

"You know," said Miss Frost, feeling for the Christmas handkerchief. "I've never had a friend like you before. I feel I could tell you anything."

"Yes, my dear. I feel the same."

"Then perhaps I should tell you. I'm older than you are. There's been talk."

"Talk?"

"Oh, I know it's not true. I don't believe it for a moment. But I should warn you. There's been talk about you and Mr. Marshall."

"Mr. Marshall!"

"Yes, my dear. I wouldn't walk with him in the garden if I were you."

"Miss Frost!"

Mrs. Dalrymple's heart was fluttering like a bird gripped by hands; but the governess's eyes were steady.

"You know what people say."

"Miss Frost! I'll ask you— I'll ask you please to go away."

The governess turned and walked into the sitting-room without a word.

"Oh."

The side door creaked behind her and the arrows of the stars found her heart.

"Oh, how could she!"

Mrs. Dalrymple was feeling sick. She walked on loose legs to the gate by the rubbish bin and leant over it, her mind numb, gazing out over the woodheap to the glassy paddocks beyond.

How long she leant there, she did not know—an eternity of pain. She was aroused by scufflings in the woodshed, and found she was shaking all over. Two figures were coming towards her in the shadow of the elms. Mrs. Dalrymple crouched down behind the rubbish-bin. They brushed past her, giggling—Elsie and Mr. Blake.

XII

The next morning their mother had a bad cold. Miss Frost made her hot lemon drinks and foments, but she refused them, whistling about her housework as if nothing was the matter with her—a faint high whistle with a trailing tail.

"Mummy," Janet said, "I think you should be in bed."

"No, no. I'm all right dear. Now I must get on with my work."

And she set about her duties with a new briskness and efficiency.

"Billy," she said, "I wish you'd wipe your boots before coming into the new room."

After dinner she and their father carried their coffee through the archway, and Mr. Marshall's eyes followed the children curiously as they trailed through to say good night.

"Ah," their father said, looking over his glasses, "very nice to be reduced to the family again!" He went less to the office now, and had set himself to re-read Dickens. The book lay open on his lap. "Pity about that cold, Josephine."

As they walked back through the sitting-room, Mr. Marshall was stretching a skein of wool.

"And if you're a good boy," Miss Frost was saying archly, "I'll knit the next pair for you."

But when her cold cleared a little, Mrs. Dalrymple was forgiving. The governess had been so good about the archway and her hot drinks.

"Frosty," she began, "I've no doubt you meant well ..."

The eyes that met hers were cold and grey.

Mrs. Dalrymple turned away haughtily. The ritual was established.

XIII

The main trouble about the move was Babs's ducks.

"But, Babs," their mother said, holding her chest and coughing, "we'll be coming back; we'll only be at grandfather's a month or two ... Oh, this wretched cough!"

It shook her lean body, paling her lips—a cough she could not shake off.

Babs's lip went down. "But Miss Frost won't feed them. They'll die, I know."

In the end the five ducks were crated and went forward with the luggage. At the station the children walked along to the brake to see them.

"See, they still know me," Babs said. "Now then, Sam, girls first."

The ducks savaged the lettuce-leaf, long coloured snake-heads through the bars of the crate.

"Look after yourself," their father said at the window. "I'm glad I insisted. Two months is too long for a cough like that. We don't want to lose her, do we?"

They kissed.

"And don't worry about me. Miss Frost can look after things."

He stood for a long time with his hat high, watching the toy train curve through the bleached paddocks.

Mr. Blake was travelling in a different compartment.

"Janet," their mother said at the junction, "I forbid you to speak to him. Mr. Blake is in disgrace."

"He doesn't seem to know," Billy said.

"That's enough, Billy. Besides, he's not even a gentleman."

Elsie had been found to be with child.

"What does a gentleman do?" Janet asked.

Mr. Blake, standing beside his golf clubs, waved. One lip curled a little as if he knew a secret. The children marched off up the platform to water the ducks.

XIV

It was early winter before they returned. Yellow leaves mottled the drive, and horses threw their heads in the frosty air.

"And to think we were in shirt-sleeves!" Billy said.

"Here's much better," from Janet.

"Oh, yes. Of course."

Miss Frost cried when she met their mother at the gate.

"You look so young," she said.

But Mrs. Dalrymple had a new composure.

"And Mr. Marshall." She took his hand. "Do you still know the names of those flowers? Oh dear, how long ago that does seem—a lifetime."

And she sighed, walking down the front path. How much smaller the house and garden seemed! A little sad, somehow, with the bare trees and blowing leaves. Almost shabby.

In the study after dinner, Doctor Dalrymple dropped his voice, nodding his head towards the archway. Through it came the murmur of two voices.

"Funny thing," he said. "Like a couple of turtles. Can't see it myself."

But his wife was stirring her coffee, smiling gently into the heart of the fire.

The Midnight Supper

I

Two Red Indians, fearful in war-paint, skulked through the fowlyard in the switch shade of young elms. A third followed at some distance, weeping, so that the tears made runnels down the paint. This was Minnie Ha Ha.

"Wait for me," she wept, holding up her pants with one fist and rubbing paint in her eyes with the other.

The two leading Indians turned and scowled for silence. That was just like Babs. She cried if she didn't come; and then she came and cried and spoilt everything. She was too young for hunting.

"Shush!" Billy hushed, jabbing at the distance with his bow. The convoy was approaching.

Pout—pout—pout.

A turkey-gobbler fanned his tail like a hand of cards, and at each strut his feathers puffed and fattened. His trembling wing-quills trailed the ground. Here was pride, green and crimson, out for a walk under a jealous sun. His serpent-hens preceded him.

"If we hit the gobbler," Billy said, "there'll be an explosion."

Janet tossed fair hair for silence.

The pageant of light-stepping birds came abreast, and the two Indians crouched low, their bows bent.

"Fire!" hissed Janet.

The arrows whispered through the winter sticks.

Oh, and it was good to see the gobbler wilt and run as they leapt out from their ambush. He was just a normal bird after all. The children's cries set the whole fowlyard in a flutter.

"Wait for me!" cried Minnie Ha Ha. But there was no waiting, for the long-necked hens were coursing through the gate, pacing for the open paddock. And Billy ran wild and fast behind, loosing his arrows.

Ping! and a turkey fell.

The children scattered back among the lean elms.

"Now you've done it," Janet said. "It was your arrow."

"You were shooting too."

Billy was pale beneath his war-paint.

"But it was your arrow."

"I wasn't aiming at it," Billy said. He was close to tears. "Where's Babs?"

They crept through elm scrub, and there in the green paddock was the turkey-hen standing up, with an arrow through its neck. Babs was coaxing it, her smock tucked up like a gleaner, crying, "Chook, chook, chook, nice chook", while the hen thrust its neck in and out, wobbling the arrow.

"Babs!" cried Billy in despair. "Come away! Oh, dear, everyone will be out in a minute."

"We could always eat it," Janet said.

"*Eat* it?"

"Why not? I love turkey. We could always chop off its head ..."

"It's certainly no use the way it is," Billy said, brightening, "with an arrow sticking through its neck. And besides, someone would be sure to see it."

And as they crept out of the elms, stalking the turkey,

60

Billy said, "It was a good shot, wasn't it, Jan?"

But the turkey, for a bird with an arrow through its throat, was surprisingly alert. They tried chook-chooking it like Babs, or sneaking up behind it while Babs chook-chooked. Each time it flapped wildly up the paddock. And the children were flushed and panting by the time they had cornered it among the elms. There, the arrow caught in saplings; and Billy, careless of the roman beak in his anxiety, tipped up its legs and tied them together with his pocket handkerchief. The legs were scaled like a lizard, and a shutter clicked shut, clicked open, over its bright little eyes.

"Shush," Billy told it.

"I'll go and get the axe," said Janet.

Up the paddock on a strong roan mare, a fat-rumped stepping mare, rode Mr. Marshall the overseer. A black kelpie sheep-dog followed in his shadow.

The three children squatted low and heard the snort and jingle as the mare shied.

"Whoa, girl!"

Mr. Marshall slapped an arched neck, tightening his knees under the roll of oilskin. The children could see red daylight in the nostrils of the mare.

"Hullo," said Marshall. "Playing redskins?"

Three meek Indians stood up screening the bird.

"Just messing about," said Billy. "Come out of it, Coil!"

But he was too late. The kelpie had dropped his tail to the line of his back and was treading with sharp-nosed caution through the elm wood. The turkey-hen gobbled, stretching its neck out along the ground. A black dog crept and was snapped in the bright lens of its eye.

"Ah!" said Marshall. He was a big curly-headed half-humorous man who turned his horse easily with strong thighs. "Scalping the turkeys, eh?"

He was at a loss whether to laugh or frown.

"I only shot an arrow in the air," Billy said loudly.

"But we know you won't tell."

Janet was at ballet school. She held out one corner of her smock, like a tea-cup.

"We know you're all right."

But no music came.

Instead, Marshall was very serious.

"You'd better let me have a look at that bird," he said, tethering the cropping mare.

Janet hung her head and bottom lip, and became a small, stained, snivelling girl.

"It was only a game," she said. "A game!"

Billy stood like stone.

"Right through the neck." Marshall hummed. He stood tall and uncertain in the winter light, looking down at the turkey. "Come out of that, Coil!"

The dog slunk sly to the mare's heels.

"Not a bad shot at all," Marshall said involuntarily.

And he was committed.

The children had him firmly by either leg while they chanted, "He won't tell! He won't tell! He won't tell! He won't tell!"

"And you'd better not tell either, Babs," Janet threatened.

The little girl drooped into tears. And Billy, wild with excitement, ran out in a wide circle like a dog just let off its chain, coming back to cry. "Right through the neck!"

"But what are you going to do with it?" said Marshall.

"Ah!" and the children became quiet with mystery.

"You'd tell Miss Frost," Janet said.

The two children shared a vision of their governess. She hovered in the chill air, middle-aged, sharp, and grey; and as she looked down at the trussed turkey a blush of anger blotched her neck, mounting inch by inch to burn on her high cheek-bones. The only rounded thing about Miss Frost was her chest; and the children believed that she kept a special stock of colour there that she could draw on when annoyed.

Marshall stole a look between the trees, hoping for a glimpse of a very different creature.

"Oh, Miss Frost wouldn't mind," he said. And, brightening, "I think she'd think it quite a lark."

The children were aghast.

"She'd kill us," said Janet, simply and with relish.

"You don't know Miss Frost," Billy said.

Marshall smiled a far-away smile—the glint of gold from some hidden seam—and said, "Oh no? At any rate, I'll keep it under my hat."

"Then," said Janet, "we're going to chop off its head—"

"And eat it," piped Billy.

"And we were wondering ..." Janet said, looking up sideways.

Marshall began to shake his head.

But within five minutes, Babs had been sent away crying and Billy held the turkey's legs behind his back while Janet stood aside, fair and detached, watching Marshall getting out his shears.

"Here," Marshall said, "you'd be no good in a branding yard. Hold it over—like that. Best put the poor thing out of its misery."

Snip!

With deep and horrified interest the children watched the headless turkey dance a dance of death.

"Why does it do that?" Janet asked.

Marshall had wiped his shears and was safe in the saddle. He turned back.

"It might be just as well ..." he said, scratching the curly hair beneath his hat, "it might be just as well if we say nothing about this. Keep it dark." And he dropped a lid and the curl of his mouth.

"You can always get round him," Janet told Billy.

The black dog followed Mr. Marshall over the hill.

II

"Sto-op it!"

The children had hidden the turkey under a cream-churn in the white-washed, ivied dairy; and now Billy was chasing Babs through the mandarin-trees with the turkey-head.

"Stop it!" Babs cried to the house.

"Billy, what are you doing?"

Miss Frost was standing full height on the verandah.

Billy ducked from tree to tree and buried the turkey-head beside the dead robin in the vegetable garden. But he had to go in for tea.

The gas-mantle glowed like a buttercup in the green warmth of the nursery. There were height-marks behind the door, showing how much they had grown, and a possum stain on the tall ceiling that sometimes looked like a fox and sometimes like a racing-car. Tonight it was a turkey.

"And where, may I ask," Miss Frost was saying, "did the turkey-head come from? It's a long while since Easter."

Billy was lost in the ceiling. He had a good idea.

He stood back from the gas-bracket and, tipping his fingers, made a silhouette on the wall. Oh, a perfect turkey-head! The turkey began to nibble at the coloured flowers of the wallpaper, to peck at a bird of paradise. Janet and Babs spilled their milk with laughter.

"Janet, you thoughtless girl!"

Slopping up the milk, Miss Frost seemed satisfied. But she looked up sharply to catch Billy frowning at Babs.

"Is that all it was, Babs?"

The little girl was aware of her strength and of her weakness. An angel-smile lit up her small round face. She tilted back the glass, blowing bubbles in the milk and kicking off her slippers under the table.

"Billy, if you're lying ..." said Miss Frost.

But Billy was ready for her.

"I didn't say anything," he said. "Even if it was a turkey-head—which I'm not saying—I didn't say it wasn't. So how could I be lying?"

"That's right." Janet nodded. "And"—daringly—"where could he get one, anyway?"

She smiled her sideways smile.

Colour began to fill up the salt cellar in Miss Frost's throat.

"Remember," she said, "I was a little girl once myself, and ..."

The three children did not hear the rest. They had put down their milk and were staring at Miss Frost. It was the silliest thing they had ever heard her say.

The silence was broken by Mr. Marshall putting his head around the door.

"Ah!" he said. "Good evening, Miss Frost. Children at tea?"

"Good evening, Mr. Marshall. Yes, they're having their tea."

She was stroking Janet's hair.

"Ah!" Marshall said, smiling.

Miss Frost smiled too; and Miss Frost had changed. The children had noticed this before when Mr. Marshall was about. She became very light on her feet and didn't seem to know what to do with things. Now, after she had wiped Babs's face, the cloth hung wet and dripping from her limp hand; and it was as if she expected Mr. Marshall to find some place to put it.

"Poor Mr. Marshall!" she said, looking at the cloth. "He's been out all day going round the little woolly lambs. You must be freezing." She shivered, hugging thin shoulders for the cold. "I've lit the bath-heater, and turned your bath on."

"Oh, good!" Marshall said. "That's good! Thank you—Miss Frost."

The children wondered why Mr. Marshall seemed so surprised, since Miss Frost turned on his bath every evening; and why he bumped into the door going out.

And in spite of the nice things she said, Billy thought that Miss Frost must be very angry with Mr. Marshall, for her neck and cheeks were stained with powdered crimson.

III

For three days the children tried to forget that there was a turkey under the cream-churn in the dairy. But each time Len came out whistling over the soft swept bricks, carrying a sun in a bucket in either hand, they were there, hidden among the hearts of the ivy-leaves, to study his face.

The ivy-leaves fluttered and sparrows flew out into the sunlight. Len blew a silver tune through his missing tooth.

"Tonight," Janet whispered, "we'll have the midnight supper."

But it wasn't as easy as all that. *Someone*, Janet said, echoing their mother, someone had to do the work!

There was the store-room to rob for raisins and sugared cherries and sweet-crusted lemon-peel; and that meant dreaming about the house until the housekeeper left her keys on the flower table. There were those flat tins of sardines among their father's fishing gear: Billy must sneak them, he was the man. Then the fire to light outside the deserted cottage in the elm wood. And of course the turkey to cook.

Billy knew all about that. You wrapped it up, feathers and all, in a jacket of black mud from the creek, and cooked it in the coals in the open, like the blackfellows do.

"All right."

The reflected fire made a brilliant window in the grey dusk among the elms, and the children were tarred with mud and dragging their feet when they met Mr. Marshall coming down from the stables.

"It's a bit blotched," Janet said, "but here's your invitation to our midnight supper."

Marshall laughed, and stopped laughing. Wouldn't they catch colds?

"Oh, it's indoors," Janet said. "In Hetherington's cottage. I didn't quite know how to spell that."

"And there'll be turkey," Billy said. "Packets of it."

Mr. Marshall was not at all sure whether he could come. He rather thought he could not.

"But you won't say anything to anyone?" Janet said.

Marshall walked off to the outside bathroom under the pepper-tree scratching his head.

IV

What did grown-ups do after dinner? It was one of the mysteries.

From their sleep-out the children could hear only the colour of conversation. A yellow square of light lit up the pot-plants far up the verandah. Miss Frost laughed in that special voice of hers and their father's voice echoed from the telephone. A possum scurried from the wistaria and across the whispering roof. Then darkness and silence for hours and hours.

"What's the matter? What's the matter?"

Billy came struggling out of his dream: they had been cooking the turkey in the bath-heater and had forgotten to turn the water on; the copper heater hissed and spat, and when finally he got to the tap only feathers came out the spout. A long face looked back at him in horror from the polished metal.

"Shush!" Janet whispered. "You'll wake up the whole house."

"Leave me alone!"

The bed was a warm wave flowing over him.

"Shush!" hushed Janet. "And you a boy! The midnight supper!"

"Oh! Oh!" Billy was out of bed. "I wasn't asleep. What's the time? Oh, it's cold."

If he could only clamber back into warm sleep!

"Shush!" Janet hissed. "You've woken them up."

They waited in breathless cold. Their father turned over and grunted, snored. The wire door squealed under their hand. And there was Babs behind them in the star-dark, belting her dressing-gown.

".Go back to bed," Janet whispered. "You're too young."

They knew what that catch and pause meant.

"All right; all right! Come along."

The three children crept over the loud boards of the verandah. They had escaped from the living and were in the land of ghosts.

Oh, the restless dark! Old Wise hooted from the black pines of the cemetery. There was a whimper among the acacias: the little boy who had fallen down the lavatory years ago. The pack on the hill bayed, bayed, and was still.

"Listen!"

The man in the cart that the housemaids heard at night was listening too. When they moved, he moved: iron wheels over the gravelled road.

"I've lost my slipper."

And that was just like Babs. She came, and spoilt everything. She hopped on one foot while they hunted the furrows of the orchard.

"Now the other one's gone. Oh, my foot's cold."

Serve her right. The children grumbled, comforted. They found the slippers; and the fire outside the cottage put out a friendly red hand to guide them. They danced with shadows round the crumbling coals.

"Now we can talk," Janet said.

Her voice seemed cupped between the elms.

"I'll bet the turkey's good. I'll bet it's just right."

Billy was raking away the coals. The top half of the turkey had burned to ash; underneath it was raw.

"Never mind," Janet said. "There's a bit here, between, that's all right. Ummmmm"—licking fatted fingers with delight.

"I'll carry it inside on the shovel," Billy said. "You go first."

Simultaneously Babs and Janet screamed.

Miss Frost crouched still among the leaping shadows.

V

There were only two ways of looking at it, Janet said. Either Miss Frost was a witch—and she certainly had behaved like one, chasing them up through the trees in the blind dark with a stinging switch of elm—or ...

It was soft morning. The children squatted in the mushroom cave of the may-bush, looking at one another. A cat curved like a long tongue past Billy's calves.

"You wouldn't think he would," Billy said. "He said to keep it dark."

Fur ran through his hand like water.

"And he was in it just as much as we were."

The cat arched, rubbed. The slant pupils of her green-gold eyes were like shade in the light of an unfocused torch.

"Perhaps"—Janet was looking at the cat—"perhaps we're being spied on."

"Go away, Tertius!"

Softly the cat sprang to the boughs of the bush. A parrot fluttered and Tertius shrank low.

"Let's walk," said Billy.

And, kicking stones down the open road, they decided what was to be done.

"If we go again, secretly, and she's not there, then

it's Mr. Marshall."

Billy nodded.

It was a desperate plan, for there was no telling whether a witch could read your thoughts. But you had to know who your friends were.

"Let's put it off till there's a moon," Billy said.

The moon frosted the twigs of the fruit-trees. And, beyond, you could imagine the road winding with no one to travel it, the creek stopped still, the paddocks blank and milky watched only by those eyes that you saw from the car at night. Anything might happen while the whole world slept. And who would know? The moon made a wicker cage of the elm wood.

The two children caught their breath.

"There's a light," Janet said. "There's a fire burning in the cottage."

Shadows crept through the darkening wood.

"Let's go back," said Billy.

Huddled together, they went on.

"We'll keep wide," Janet said, "opposite the window."

Flames leapt on the high walls. And yet a window is a comforting sight. They moved like foxes to the edge of the light; and, tiptoe, peered in.

In the firelight Miss Frost sat on Mr. Marshall's knee.

Back in the moonlit orchard, panting, Janet began to giggle.

"What are you laughing at?" Billy said. "That doesn't prove anything."

"He was kissing her," Janet said. "Don't you see?"

"Well?"

"Oh, you're too young."

"I still think she's a witch," Billy said. "And she's got Mr. Marshall under her spell."

And, looking up at the brilliant moon, he half expected to see the governess and the overseer slide by on a broom of elm.

VI

The next evening the children ran wild with a primitive kind of excitement.

There were two bathrooms: the real one, tall, scrubbed, shadowy; and the hot round world reflected in the bath-heater, where points of light glowed and plump bronze children played like young gods.

Warm and flushed from the towel, they ran to the nursery. And there, while the fire threw up their shadows, they danced their dance-undressed.

It was danced in dressing-gowns round the table. Round and round they went, Janet light and fair, Billy sturdy, and Babs a tiny kicking colt. And when they were puffed, giddy, they flung their dressing-gowns wide and danced the final measure with nothing on except their flying capes. Fat young shadows danced with them on the wall.

"What is the meaning of this?"

Crabbed age stood in the doorway. The children tumbled, giggling, to the couch.

"I won't have it," Miss Frost said, her colour rising. "You should be ashamed of yourselves."

But the children were not ashamed. They giggled all the more; until Janet brought a sudden silence on the room by saying, "Miss Frost, why is Mr. Marshall so funny these days; you know, kind of not here?"

Miss Frost's face was scarlet, but surprisingly she smiled.

"Have you noticed it?" she said. And archly, "Perhaps Mr. Marshall has been hit by one of Cupid's darts."

"Who's he?" said Billy.

"Oh, he's a naughty little boy with a bow and arrow who shoots people through the heart and makes them fall in love."

"Wouldn't it hurt?" Billy said.

Miss Frost giggled.

"Oh no, it doesn't hurt. They like it. And now, off to bed with you."

Miss Frost turned out the light and a bat started flitting around the orange-tree with a sound like the snip, snip, of a pair of scissors. Billy sat up on his elbow.

"I wonder, Jan," he said, "if that little boy could hit a turkey?"

"Well," said Janet, "he got Mr. Marshall in the neck."

But after they had been scolded for laughing, she lay in bed and sobbed for a long time before she went to sleep.

The Fire-engine

The morning the fire-engine came the two children were in trouble for forgetting to clean their teeth. Instead, they stole out by the side verandah, and by the time the wire door told behind them, they were beyond hearing, racing like young lambs across the misty horse-paddock.

Miss Frost stood by the door and called for the last time.

"I shall not call again!" she cried.

But the children were lost in the shifting mist, in the shrouded bulk of the elms; and all she saw in the fairy sunlight were their green footprints crossing the opal sheen of the clover. Miss Frost held her throat a moment and felt it burning. She was upset; her whole day was in tatters. With a flux of pleasure she rehearsed their return for lunch.

At the front gate, panting, the children studied the wheel-tracks.

"No, it's not come yet," Janet said. "That's the mailman."

"How do you know," said Billy, "that the fire-engine hasn't the same sort of wheels?"

With his fingers he gathered up seams of mud where tyres had laid down a fresh mould in clay.

"I just know," Janet said. "Fire-engines have big wheels."

She climbed up on a gate-post, arranged her skirts, and waited. With the clay Billy began modelling a fireman's helmet.

"I still think it might be it," he said. "I think we ought to go down to the dam and see." For the fire-engine was to pump out the waterhole for cleaning.

"Don't be silly," Janet said, so Billy climbed up on the other gate-post and waited, too. The mist sagged with light along the road; great red hands of river-gums tore out patches of blue; a rainbow lay down across the clover. At last ("Oh, look, Jan!") the sun itself came bouncing along the road through the mist.

"There it is! There it is!" cried Billy; and Janet forgot to say "Told you", and said instead, "Come over onto my post, Billy." For girls are so made that they enjoy themselves better when they are close to someone.

"See it shine!" Billy cried, clambering up beside her. "I'll bet it's as big as a house."

For at a distance the fire-engine made a brave show. The sunlight waved flags in its brasswork, and streamers of mist peeled from the painted navy, red, and gold. For a moment it held its splendour, the thing itself, awaking images of night-skies flushed with flame. The children sat in awe. Then the mists cleared, and the fire-engine rattled round the turn, as comical as a very old train. It had high spoked wheels and a low square bonnet, and three men sat straight-backed and melancholy on the perched driving-bridge.

"They're not even wearing helmets," said Billy in dismay; but Janet was giggling so infectiously that he forgot his disappointment and joined her in mockery.

"Just old porters' caps."

"And so serious!" Janet's voice was shrill with laughter. "As if—oh, dear—it was Christmas Day."

The fire-engine shook to a stop before the gate, and the children struggled with their laughter.

"Well, aren't you going to open the gate?" said the driver, and he blew the siren.

The driver was Mr. Pringall, bland and pompous, and the siren was not a real siren. It was too much for the children. They were shaken by agonies of laughter and shyness. Janet swivelled on the post and cried into her dress, while Billy, slipping down and averting his face, opened the gate. He leant over the gate, and the fire-engine drove through, past their quivering backs.

"Well, what's so funny?" Mr. Pringall said—which sent them into new smothers of laughter.

"Must be a comic, eh, Albie? Never knew I was so funny. Real Little Tich!" And he cocked his hat on the side of his head and pulled humorous grimaces. With gasps of relief the children stopped laughing.

"We weren't laughing at you," Janet said. "We were laughing at something completely different." She climbed with composure from the post. "Where do you want to go?" Immediately they started laughing again.

"Always up to some stupid tricks," said the young man on the right. He was broad-shouldered, with dark finger-waved hair and a fine nose, and, until he spoke, they did not take him for the dopey youth who used to clean the boots and was sacked for calling Miss Frost by her Christian name. They liked him for that, and were sorry they had treated him so badly, putting chaff in his hat, and frogs' eggs in his tea, and pushing open the lavatory door while he was inside. Now here he was on a fire-engine—and Janet knew a new shame. His name was Bob Simpson.

76

"Stupid yourself," she said.

"Well, this isn't getting the dam pumped out," said Mr. Pringall. "All aboard and we'll get under way."

And as they clambered up on the back Billy whispered, "There, I told you! It has the same wheels as the mailman."

II

At the waterhole the firemen became very busy, stripping off their coats and rummaging in the belly of the fire-engine for overalls and rubber boots. As they buttoned on the overalls, they faced one way, gazing out into the mists of the valley; and Janet scanned the hills behind. They stamped about a moment, getting the feel of the boots. The day was warming and it was a pleasant change to be out in the country.

"All set?" Mr. Pringall cried. "I think we'll back her in here, Albie."

The dam was small, with a grassed holding-bank on the lower side where the children sometimes picnicked while they fished for yabbies. During the summer it had dried up, but the autumn rains had begun before Sol got around to cleaning it with a scoop and draught-horses. Now the fire-engine backed down to the edge of the water, the wheels were chocked, and great canvas hoses were unwound from it. Albie waded out into the dam with the strainer of the suction-hose cupped in his hands. The other two stood back in their gum-boots giving advice.

"Well out, Albie!" they shouted. "More to the right, Albie! Look out or the water will be over the top of your boots!"

Then, turning to Billy without lowering his voice, Mr. Pringall said, "It's no use talking to Albie; he's deaf as a post."

Stooped over the strainer, Albie looked up from the centre of the dam, and a half-moon grin rounded his seamless face.

"How will that do?" he said in a whisper.

"Right!"

Mr. Pringall worried the gears to pump, and a head of water coursed down the delivery hose, leaving a dozen silver fountains in its wake. Bob walked down the hose, laying flat stones over the leaks. When he came to the last hole he put his boot on it and rolled a cigarette.

"Going to be a nice day," he said.

Finally he laid a stone over that, too, and joined Mr. Pringall and the children on the clovered bank. The mists swirled and thinned, the sky turned the muddy waterhole to blue. It was as if they were at the centre of a pearl. Nothing existed but the bank and the dam and Albie, deaf and mute, rising out of the water. The fire-engine throbbed like the heart of the world. They stretched out idly in the sun, and Janet, edging over, leant her back against Bob's knee. After a time Billy threw a stone into the dam, splashing Albie.

"Don't do that," Mr. Pringall said. "Albie's working. Somebody's got to keep the thing going, or the strainer gets blocked."

The dam was almost empty. Albie fossicked in the mud with one hand and threw a piece of rag on the bank. Billy washed it at the outlet pipe and found it was one of his cloth hats. He put it on and danced in the sunlight.

"It's mine," he said. "I wondered where it'd got to."

"There's something else, Albie!" Mr. Pringall shouted. "Over there!"

Albie followed the direction of his finger and, resting the strainer on the toe of his boot, reached over for a second piece of cloth. Immediately Janet saw it she sprang up crying, "Throw it to me, Albie! Albie, do you hear?"

But Albie did not hear. Methodically he rinsed it in the shallow water at his feet and, stretching it wide between his hands, grinned seamlessly. He held a pair of girl's cotton bloomers.

"Ah!" said Mr. Pringall. "Now, who would they belong to?" while Bob smirked his sly smile.

"You're mad, you're all mad!" cried Janet suddenly. "I wish you were all dead!"

And turning she ran wildly down the valley. Stumbling through the mist, she heard the laughter of the men following her.

III

Billy stayed to help the firemen roll up the gear. When he crept in for lunch, he was surprised to find Miss Frost and Janet seated at either end of the sofa and all Janet's dolls spread out on the seat between them. Miss Frost did not seem annoyed; in fact, he had never seen Janet and their governess quite so friendly before. Good, he thought, she must have forgotten; so, pocketing his hands for his best swagger, he said, "You should have seen—"

"Get out," said Janet. "We don't want boys in here."

"You'll find your lunch in the pantry," Miss Frost said. "And I'll speak to you later about your teeth."

"But the fire-engine," Billy said. "Gee, it was a dotty old thing!"

"No such thing," said Janet. "It was a lovely fire-engine."

Billy walked out and ate his lunch alone in the pantry.

The Haunted Cradle

Soon after Mr. Blake left, Bob Simpson saw the ghost in a stroke of lightning. The storm that day had lifted the roof of the barn, and riding home to town after work in the dark, he saw the lightning run through it, and there was the ghost perched high amongst the streaming rafters.

"What was it like?" Billy said.

"Well, that doesn't matter much," Bob said. "It was the pipe that got me in. A man could be mistaken in the flash, like; but you can't get away from that pipe."

For the ghost had a pipe in its mouth, and even after the lightning Bob could see the glow and fade of it against the windy dark. And listening to him by the cottage fire, his chest half bare, his nose a hooked shadow, and a cocksure droop to his young eyes, the children thought that it must have been a terrible sight to have frightened him so much; because Bob galloped back to the homestead and refused to go home for a week.

He had his meals in the kitchen, except lunch which Elsie cut for him; and at night he camped for comfort in a little bare room between the cook's room and Elsie's. But at the end of the week he was looking more frightened than ever.

Their father had to speak to him finally; and although he laughed about it later, saying Bob was like a ghost himself, he was serious at the time; and Bob rode home looking sulky and making an elaborate circle round the barn. But when the barn was pulled down and a convict's skeleton was found under the red-box corner-post, the slow, self-confident curl returned to his lip end.

Soon after that Bob and Elsie were married and went to live in the cottage up the creek. And the children, returning from their holiday, rode off through the ram paddock and the yellow willows to hear all about the ghost. At first Bob did not seem to remember very much, but gradually his memory improved, and each day there was some new and exciting detail he had forgotten.

"Did he have a sheet over him?" Billy said.

"Sheet? Oh, yes, he had a sheet over him. My oath!"

They were sitting on the weatherboard verandah under the shingles, watching the long autumn day flare out in the willows. Bob had his bare arm round Elsie's waist and he gave her a squeeze.

"That's right," he said, "isn't it?"

"Get on with you." Elsie wriggled her heavy shoulders and giggled. "The things you say? It's not right. Well, one more cake all round and then you kids better hop it."

She seemed upset quite suddenly, her fair, downy cheeks flushing a little; but as she walked through to get the cakes from the enamelled tin with the gold roses on it, her eyes looked back into Bob's as if joined to them by wires. Her face had an unreal lustre as if it had been glazed with icing.

"There you are," Bob said, "you've got your cakes.

82

Now slide off, vanish."

"We haven't finished yet." Billy was cleaning the paper cone over his finger. "This is the best part."

But Bob and Elsie had walked through together into the yellow hallway.

"You know," Billy said, "Elsie's changed. Her chin doesn't wobble any more."

The willow-leaves dropped into the coiling water.

"Do you think it was a real sheet?"

They were riding home, back on the subject of the ghost. It seemed more real than ever amongst the shouldering shadows.

But they soon learnt not to mention it in front of their mother.

"There was no ghost," she said, gathering up her mending. "There are no such things as ghosts; and it would never have happened if I had been there. I refuse to have anything to do with it. Nothing from this house will go there, and I forbid you children to speak to Elsie."

And she walked out of the room without looking at their father.

But this only kept their interest alive; and, forgetting her warning, they called at the cottage as often as possible. In fact she had given them an idea, and when nobody was about, they struggled down the hill and under the willows with broken chairs from the box-room and broken saucepans that Bob mended in the evenings. The pine kitchen closed in around the furniture, and there were always pink cakes in the enamel tin by the fire.

"Here you are," Elsie said, "take two."

For some reason her smile was more honeyed now, less free and friendly; and she stuffed cakes into their pockets when they did not want them.

"Go on," she said, "they won't bite you. What have you done with your appetites today?"

"Don't overdo it, Else," Bob told her. "They'll eat no tea when they get home, and then where will you be?"

He was lying back on one of the verandah chairs, sharing a joke with himself.

"Yes, sulphur," he said. "There was a terrible smell of sulphur. Of course, the mare was snorting and chiv-vying around like she was flank-roped, but I smelt it all the same. You know, like the smell around the dip at dipping-time. Dries the nose."

His descriptions were more detailed, less convincing, now, but the children hardly noticed the change. They were taken up with furnishing a real house. It was far more exciting than any game they had ever played; and, as Elsie fawned and they dimly sensed their power, they began to look upon it almost as their own.

"I know," Billy said as they waded through the creek with a three-legged washstand. "Why don't we wait till they're all in town and take a dray-load? There's packets of it there—just lying about."

"No."

Janet set the tiled top down on the sand. The tiles were green with naked pink tulips in their centres. "No, this way is best." And she pushed back a lock of fair hair. "Do you know, last time we were there I don't think Elsie had swept out the lavatory!" She spoke in a high concerned way with a little frown between her eyes. "Your turn for the top."

"I still think ..." Billy said, the tiled edge biting his heel, "I still think a dray-load would be better."

"No." Janet was quite decided. "It's not ours, real-ly—but it's a long way to carry things. And it takes longer."

The furnishing was well on the way when quite suddenly Elsie went to town and came back at the end of the week with a baby. The children were delighted.

"There are those things of Babs's in the ottoman," Janet said. "Aren't you thrilled? Now we've got a baby!"

"I'd rather have a cattle-pup myself," Billy said.

"Don't be silly. Now count them—three, four, five, six. That ought to do for a start. Spread the sheet back. Oh, I'm dying to see it!"

But when they ran up the green slope through the quince hedge, things were not as they expected at all. The baby was all right—a pink sugar-pig with a strangely old face, sleeping the winter away in a bag cradle of cross-stays; but the house was a pigsty and Elsie was bloated with crying.

"Thank you, I'm sure."

She was only composed while she sat by the baby, aimlessly rocking the cradle and tickling its belly with a ripe forefinger.

"She knows me," she said. "See, she knows her mummy."

The baby howled.

Janet began tidying up the house, and at five Bob came in. Bob had changed, too. He had lost his lidded look, and all the upward lines of his face had vanished so that he seemed five years younger. But his eyes worried Janet most. They really looked as if they had seen a ghost.

And so it was all winter, except that as Bob grew more surly Elsie cheered up. Each time the children called the house was more untidy and Elsie sat by the cradle screwing up her eyes and making bubble sounds through fat lips. Sometimes she swept a stroke of dust out into the wind, but it blew back, gilding the shaft of wintry light from the window.

"There you are," she said. "You can't do nothing with it. That's what I tell him, but men are that particular!"

And she returned to stare entranced at the fire where water boiled over, blackening the live coals.

"She's that fair," she said. "I thought she would be."

Janet was so upset she grew pale and tired, and her mother began to worry about her.

"I don't know what's come over Janet," she said. "She's riding too much."

But Janet only got impatient.

"The house," she told Billy. "It was so nice. Oh, Elsie's just a pig ... Poor Bob!"

Then, finding Elsie submissive, she recovered her spirits. There were days of elaborate spring-cleaning, sweeping out nails and wax matches from the bedroom, folding clothes back into suitcases, and carrying boxes choked with rubbish to burn in the wind. At these times she was exalted, and she stood with her fair head on one side, arranging jonquils in a jam-jar, moving a green stem here, and stepping back to consider, while Elsie, fat and mild, hung around with a broom, ready to take orders as if she was a housemaid again. But she would disappear and they would find her sitting by the cradle. Janet was very high-handed with her, setting her to scrub the kitchen floor.

"If you can't leave it for a minute!" she said. "Don't you want the house to look nice for Bob?"

But as the sunlight crept in she made it up to Elsie, finding new reasons to stay, and wandering from room to room, from window to window, to gaze out across the winter paddocks. When Bob came in, she watched him through her lashes, negligently smiling; but he never noticed the difference, trailing his cowyard oilskin across the scrubbed floor.

So she grew silent once more and the house was never finished and they always ended up round the fire, eating cakes and talking about the ghost.

The ghost interested them again now because Bob would not talk about it. Instead, he shook his head and smiled rawly as if the thought of it troubled him, which of course increased the mystery. But Elsie encouraged Billy, giggling and inciting his smiles and remembering all the little details that had grown up during the early months of their marriage.

"I wonder if it really had a sheet over it," Billy said.

"He wasn't in a state to know." Elsie laughed. "But here he is; you ask him."

Bob was coming in with his oilskin blowing, slamming the door on the gale.

"Crows are terrible this year," he said. "There was one chasing a ewe all over the paddock—a full-grown ewe!"

"Did the ghost have a sheet over it, Bob?"

"Ghost? There wasn't any ghost."

And he stood for some time looking down at the baby before squatting on his heel by the fire.

"There's an old pram," Janet said. "We'll bring you a pram next time, Bob."

Perhaps he just did not like the cradle.

It was while they were wheeling the pram over that they found St. John's tombstone in the willow; and because of the ghost and the skeleton, they were prepared to believe anything.

The pram had run well downhill, but it was rough going among the tussocks and Babs refused to get out.

"I'm tired," she said. "I feel sick."

"If you don't get out," Billy said, "I'll tip you over the bank into the creek."

"And I'll tell."

"You won't be here to tell," Janet said. "You'll be floating down the waterfall."

They had stopped under a cloven willow that made a new green cage for the magpies; and looking up, they saw a six-inch chip of white willow-wood let into the seamed bark. It was carved deeply with the point of a knife.

ST JOHNS WART
KILLED HERE
17TH DECEMBER

"Read it again, Jan."

Janet read it. And the children stood dumbfounded under the tree, the shadows suddenly cunning, the blue day strange and withdrawn outside.

"What do you think it means?"

"Well," Janet said, "I expect it means just what it says. Someone was killed and buried here last year. On the seventeenth."

Babs took Janet's hand, and Billy glanced through the green bars of the willow with a pleasant feeling of panic.

"But what's the Wart doing?" he said. "You don't

suppose they just cut his wart off and buried that?"

He was relieved to find that he could laugh at such a time, and Babs stopped dragging at Janet's hand and looked up at her, ready to smile.

"Like the one Billy had on his knee?"

"That's his surname," Janet said. She had become very sure of herself during the past few months, and their laughter made up her mind. "If you want to make a joke of it—right here where he's buried..." Illogically, the murdered saint had assumed for her the drawn features of Bob Simpson.

"But who would murder him?"

"Well," Janet said, "Mr. Blake left in December—and in a great hurry."

And she made off along the bank while Billy followed with the pram and Babs stumbled amongst the tussocks, crying, "Wait for me!"

Elsie was no help. She just sat rocking the fat baby and saying, "Well, I never! Well, I never did!"

"We'll have to wait till Bob comes in," Janet said.

She stood aloof by the window, watching the wind shake the first delicate buds of the quince-trees. They were like little breasts amongst the curling leaves. Sometimes she had to lean right over the sill to stop herself smiling at Billy's silly stories about buried warts; but when she rushed out and Bob laughed too, it was too much for her pride.

"Oh, that!" he said. "It's a weed, a noxious weed. Blake and I salted a patch there and left that to mark the tree."

"See!" Billy laughed. "She thought a saint had been buried."

"It says St. John."

"St-John's-wort's a weed."

And Bob lifted his eyebrows and laughed openly for the first time for months.

"Silly kids!"

Janet was furious.

"It says killed; why should you write killed? Oh, you just won't talk. You're frightened—like you are of the ghost."

They were in the kitchen now, and Elsie was rocking the baby to a fro.

"He's frightened of the ghost, anyway."

Elsie began to smirk, but Bob put his coat down quietly.

"There was no ghost," he said. "Get that. And there's no ghost in this house, either. But"—and he picked up the chip of wood—"if I ever catch up with that chap Blake, I'll murder him. I will. Murder him."

The chip cracked between his great hands, and, as if released, his anger flowed out.

"And now get out!" he shouted. "Stupid, prying, half-baked bloody kids! Clear out! That goes for you too, Else, if you like."

"And take your broken chairs with you!" he cried from the door, pitching one into the hedge.

"And your pram!"

"And your bloody washstand!"

His voice followed them on the wind, and the chairs swayed amongst the quince-blossom like giant birds.

They waited for some time for Elsie by the creek, but she did not come.

"We were only trying to help him," Billy said.

He complained and argued all the way home, but though she was very pale, Janet said nothing. She did not even answer back when Billy laughed at her about St-John's-wort; and when he spoke about the ghost, she said simply, like Bob, "There wasn't a ghost."

"How do you know?"

"I half knew all the time. Oh, we've been fools."

That was all she would ever say about it, and for months she would not go near the cottage. Then one day they were passing and Elsie called them in to see the new furniture.

It was plywood, varnished, all nice and new from the store, and the baby had a new cot with new bead-panels in it, and Elsie laughed all the time; and they ate pink cakes on the verandah just as they had in the first days of her marriage. But when Bob came in, it was different. He sat for a while and laughed a little, too, but the children left soon after. The only way Billy could ever explain the change was that he had grown up; and when he and Elsie spoke about the garden, she seemed grown-up too, as if the little flower-bed by the step had some special, serious meaning for them.

"Don't pull the tops off," Elsie said.

As they were going, she called Janet back.

"Tell your mum," she said, "we're having another baby. Just say that. I'd like her to know."

"Don't forget," she called from the hedge.

"Let's gallop," Billy said.

But Janet wouldn't. She rode home by the creek where the willow leaves were falling again into the water.

The Button and
the Heretic

The children were up in the yellow-and-purple elm.
The way you got there was very simple: you followed
the possum-tree. The possum-tree was a wistaria-vine.
It crawled out from under the house, strangled a verandah post, clambered over the hot iron roof, and leapt
up into the overhanging branches.

Billy, swinging hand over hand, dropped one to his
side and said, "Look, Jan! I'm hanging by one arm."

"Shut up," Janet said. "I'm thinking about God."

She sat in the fork of the money-box bough, her
dress tucked up and her tail hanging down, and gazed
out through hops and the grape-like clusters of the
vine. Down in the mists of the creek the windmill
clanged and a cuckoo sang his seven notes.

"You can't think of Him all the time," Billy said.
"Have you got the money?"

"Yes."

And Janet opened her hand.

Her hand was mottled from her grip and the money
was sticky—threepence, two pennies, two halfpennies,
and a button, that they had found sewn in the corner of
a sitting-room curtain.

"The button's no good," Billy said. "The button's
no use at all."

"Oh, yes, it is," Janet said. "Think of finding a
treasure and just one button with it!"

She gazed at it in her palm as if she had never seen a button before in her life. It was shiny-brown and had four eyes in it: an Army button.

"I think you're mad," Billy said. "Who'd want a button?"

"You don't know what they might want. It might be two hundred years! Think of chopping down a tree and finding a button two hundred years old!"

"Oh, all right," Billy said. "I'd rather find threepence myself. I'd just throw the silly old button away. But come on."

He pulled a dead branch like a cork out of the limb, and there was an astonishing little hole like a mouth saying oh!

"One at a time, Jan."

Janet rolled a penny down her finger into the hole, and they heard it rattle along the hollow into the great black cavern of the bole.

"You can hear it all the way down," Billy said. "Like Les Craig drinking tea."

The threepence made a threepenny sound, and then the button went down.

"Did you hear it?" Janet said. "It ran best of all."

And the children sat silent under the mysterious leaves, Billy thinking of the treasure and the surprise of its discoverers—in how many years' time? Perhaps they would be dead. No one would know how it came to be there in the butt of an elm. Yellow hops fell down like money all round him, and the cuckoo called from a faraway world in the mist.

But Janet was thinking of the button lying there all alone in the dark with nothing to see through its four little eyes. She had been moody since hearing of Elsie's second baby and now she became very sad indeed. The elm-hops were buttons for her, and the cuckoo made bright buttons of the air, but her own particular button, the only button that she loved in all the world, was gone. Never, never, never ...

A tear-drop started in her eye, hung on the lid and rolled like a button into her lap.

"Are you thinking about God now?" Billy said.

"Yes."

Janet tossed her fair hair and another tear from her nose.

"I'll bet you're not. I'll bet you're thinking about that silly old button!"

"I'm not—and it's not silly. I'm thinking about God. Miss Frost says you've got to think about God all the time."

"Why?"

"So you'll go to heaven, of course."

And quite suddenly Janet saw the whole thing. It was as simple as that, as simple as their money-box bough. Away you rolled like a button into the dark hollow that was death; then God came along with his axe and chopped you out. And in a vision she saw her button climb like an eagle up a shaft of sunlight and disappear into the vague blue of heaven.

"If you're not careful," she said cryptically to Billy, "no one will come along and chop you out at all."

Billy made nothing of this; he was impatient of such fantasies. Chopping out was not the point.

"You can't think of Him all the time," he said, gazing up into the thumbnail leaves. "How about when you're asleep at night?"

"You dream, don't you?"

"How about ..." Billy was craning his neck up still farther. "How about when you're sitting on the pot?"

"Now you're being rude," Janet said. "God'll hear you and pay you out. You see!"

But Billy was shinning out along the branch, delighted with his remark, and shaking bough-loads of hops down on to Len's raked paths.

"Hey! What are you up to up there?" a voice cried out from the green well below.

"They've got to fall sometime, Len," Billy said. "Haven't they, Jan?"

"I tell you," Janet said, "I'm thinking about God."

"I'll give you something to think about if you keep shaking them hops down," Len shouted.

He had walked out into the sunlight and stood gazing up, a short, lean Devonshireman with wild blue eyes. The bone of his nose and jaw made white highlights through the skin, and he wore outsize boots to mask his tiny feet.

"He's really wild," Billy said. "Look how white he's gone."

"Len," Janet said, "why do your boots turn up?"

"You'll know all about my boots if you don't come down out of that."

"*If* we come down, you mean. They're pretty big, but they wouldn't reach this far."

Billy laughed hops down all over Len, who cried, "By God!" and, kneeling down, began to take a boot off.

"I always wanted to see his foot," Janet said.

Len laced his boot up again and shouted, "Any more from you and I'll hose you out, that's what!"

White-eyed, the children looked at one another.

"We won't shake any more *hops* down," Billy said; and when the sound of raking began below again, he leaned far out on the bough and rolled a shilling of spit down into the pan of Len's hat. Len wrenched the hat off and scuttled like a crab for the garden-bed. But the children were racing, too—down the limb with arms wide, around the bole and hand over hand along the vine to the roof. As Billy let go and his feet felt the heat of the iron, a clod of clay spun past him and broke into dust on the ridge.

"That's done it," he said. "They'll all be out."

Sliding down the far side, another clod burst between them—for Len had been a grenade-thrower in France; then doors were banging and people were shouting; and they slid down the guttering past the kitchen window into the rubbish bin, and were away around the pepper-tree and the well to the lavatory by the dairy.

It was an old outside family-lavatory covered with ivy, and with three holes of different sizes for father, mother, and child—a kindly place of old newspapers and winter flies.

The children slammed the door, wrenched down their pants, and sat there hearing in the distance Miss Frost's voice crying, "Jannnn-et! Billl-y!" in just that high tone that meant bed without supper or their father's razor-strop.

"I expect we're safe here," Billy said.

"They couldn't come in while we're doing something." Janet was quite shocked. "Even Len wouldn't dare."

"I got him a good one, didn't I?"

"Oh ... not bad."

Billy waited till his heart stopped beating, and then he said, "Are you still thinking about God, Jan?"

Immediately Janet's eyes looked far away through the knots in the door and she said, "Yes, of course, I am."

"Were you thinking of Him all the time?"

"Yes."

"Even when you fell in the rubbish bin?"

"I don't have to tell you everything," Janet said. "I needn't tell you anything if I don't want to. You're not God."

But Billy, sitting in the centre seat and laughing down at his pants dangling from his bare toes, felt at that moment that he knew something of the mystery and delight of godhead.

Apples and Pears

I

Usually on Sundays the Grants came to their place. The first they saw of the Grants was an eddy of white dust moving along the saddle of Bald Hill against the pale rim of the sky. The eddy disappeared into trees, and a black ant crept out from the trees and down the white road into the valley. For ten minutes after that it was guesswork—Mr. Grant pulling on the brass outside-brake in your mind, and Guy Grant, pale and tidy, leading the avenue gate open and leading it shut again. At last the car itself came splashing through the sunlight between the elms, with Guy holding a model aircraft out in the wind.

Usually, too, there was something new about the Grants' car—a coat of paint, a brass spotlight, or a new-type carburettor under the low bonnet; and Guy had a new propellor on his biplane. Their father stood gazing with his hands on his hips while Mr. Grant laid open the bonnet; their mother and Mrs. Grant walked down the path, both talking and laughing lightly together about the things that had worried them all the week; and Janet and Billy and Babs looked at one another while Guy spun the propellor of his plane.

"Well, Les," their father said, "you'll have to get yourself another car soon. There doesn't seem to be much more you can fit on this one."

"With the price of petrol the way it is," Mr. Grant said, "I won't be able to afford this one much longer."

Mr. Grant called petrol pe-trol; and while he clipped back the brass catches on the bonnet, their father laughed heartily at his own remark and the children looked harder at one another because of Mr. Grant's pronunciation.

"You brought your clubs, Les?"

Mr. Grant reached into the back of the car and brought out a bagful. The heads of the irons were polished and the woods reared up in the bag like the heads of cobras. Their father had his set leaning by the gatepost—half a dozen clubs in a stovepipe of canvas. And he and Mr. Grant set off for the three-hole links in the horse-paddock, their father striding, lean and tall, with Mr. Grant a sandy bantam-weight beside him.

Mr. Grant called golf go-lf. He addressed the ball seriously with a quick preliminary tremor of the clubhead and a tremor of the shoulders, like a cat shaking meat. The ball climbed to a pinhead, banked, and curved over towards the willows by the creek. He addressed their father seriously, too. Their father joked about winds high up, and played quietly down the centre of the flat, his ball bouncing over the cow-pats on the short cropped grass. But he became serious himself whenever Mr. Grant was in front.

When Mr. Grant was in front their father smoothed out the hoof-marks on the gravel green with his putter and Mr. Grant stood seriously on one leg with the other leg to the side. Guy stood in his shadow with his leg out too and the heavy bag of clubs over his shoulder. As the ball approached the hole, Mr. Grant leant forward, helping it in, and Guy leant back, keeping it out.

"Good putt, Doctor. A very long putt."

"Well, Les, that approach shot of yours was as good as I've seen."

Janet and Billy found it very dull. They stamped along the creek bank, sending landslides of cracked earth toppling down into the clear coils of water, or played golf with willow boughs, hitting cow-pats onto the greens.

"Here now, Billy, what do you think you're up to?"

"Come on, Guy," Janet called. "Come and play"—calling in her longest, weariest voice.

Guy liked to watch his father. But sometimes he handed over the bag of polished clubs, and the children ran wild. They raced away across the pad-docks, playing chasings, leaving Guy far behind. They took him into their underground cave in the creek bank and blew out the jam-tin lamp. They climbed the giant pear-tree growing wild by the first tee, looking for sparrows' eggs. Guy stood underneath amongst the irises, gazing up: a slight, pale boy with a fringe of fair hair, in a white shirt and long short pants.

"Look, Jan. Look at them all," Billy said. "One two three four five. And aren't they speckled? Feel! They're still warm. See, Guy"—holding a sparrow's egg in sunlight between his thumb and finger.

"I've got a collection at home," Guy said, "of all the birds' eggs in the world."

"I'll bet you haven't."

"I'll bet I have. I'll show you."

"You wouldn't have an ostrich egg," Janet said.

"I've got an emu egg."

"I'll bet you haven't got as many eggs as we have."

"Yours are all sparrows' eggs," Guy said. "Anyone can get sparrows' eggs."

100

"Then why don't you come up and get them, then?"

"I've got enough sparrows' eggs," Guy said.

There was a pause while the children gazed down through the leaves of the pear-tree and Guy gazed up at them.

"See this tree," Billy said. "You think it's a pear-tree, don't you? Well, it grows apples as well."

"It couldn't," Guy said. "Look, they're all pears."

Hard green pears hung down from the branches.

"It does," Billy said, "sometimes. It grew one last summer. Didn't it, Jan?"

Janet was looking into the sparrows' nest, but her head seemed to nod.

"It couldn't," Guy said.

"I tell you," Billy said, getting excited, "it grew an apple. A big red juicy apple. I ought to know, I ate it. Didn't I, Jan?"

"Yes," Janet said, "he ate it."

"A pear-tree couldn't grow an apple," Guy said, standing with his feet apart. "I've read about them."

"It's all very well reading," Billy said. "You didn't eat the apple."

He and Janet both laughed.

"It was last summer," Billy said. "Janet climbed right up to the very top of the tree, and there it was growing in amongst the pears, and she picked it."

"I said I found the apple up the tree," Janet said. "I said I picked it."

"She probably picked it somewhere else," Guy said, "and had it in her pocket."

"I didn't have it in my pocket," Janet said.

"There you are, Guy. You're mad. You won't believe anything you're told."

"Let's climb down," Janet said, "and go for a walk."

They straggled down the hill in the cooling sunshine to the creek. Willows wept over the steep bank, and dropped a leaf here, a leaf there, that turned to fish in the gold water, dragging tiny sun-pointed shadows over the gravel. They could hear their father and Mr. Grant talking half a mile away up the flat.

"Look!" Janet cried suddenly. "Look, a landslide!"

And when they turned to look, she pushed Guy over the bank into the creek.

After that the Grants went home early in case Guy caught a cold, and the children were sent to bed in the late afternoon. Cocks crowed and blowflies still buzzed at the wire gauze behind the yellow blinds.

"But I'm not sorry I did it," Janet said. "He's such an awful liar. All the birds' eggs in the world, and not even an ostrich egg!"

II

The next Sunday they visited the Grants' place for a change. Their father backed the Brazier out under the black pine by the garden gate and sat in the car, occasionally pushing back the peak of his cap and squeezing the rubber horn. The children watched him from their ponies behind the woodheap. They saw their mother hurrying up the path, pausing here and there to snip flowers for Mrs. Grant. The car stalled, and started off down the avenue with a spit of gravel. The children turned their ponies and galloped off down the paddock, taking the short cut around Bald Hill.

Quinces hung like green moons among the dim leaves by the Simpsons' cottage, but there was no time for stopping. As they climbed the rise, dust blew through the stringybarks, chalking the sky ahead.

"It's no use," Billy said. "We'll never beat the car when Babs is with us."

"Dad's driving fast," Janet said. "He always does when mum's late."

"What's the hold-up?" Billy said, looking at an imaginary watch.

"Come on, Babs!"

Babs was still far away down the sheep-pad, clinging to the pommel like a monkey, her legs flapping straight out at the sides. Midget cantered on stiff joints, kicking a hoof to the side.

"I dropped my hat," Babs said, panting. "It came off back there by the salt-trough."

When they finally rode over the rise, they could see the Grants' place through the trees. It had a gabled roof like a dolls' house, a square of English garden, roses and pebble paths. Ranges leant above it, blue or spiked with ringbarked trees, the wild hills of kangaroos and eagles' nests.

"I'll tell you what," Janet said. They were riding down the white road in the sunshine. "Let's take our saddles off. Let's gallop down there bareback."

"That's a good idea," Billy said. "Aren't we too close, though?"

"We could always swing off the road and leave them behind a tree."

"That's a good idea. And sneak back on the way home when they've gone inside."

They turned off and dismounted under a giant blue-gum. The day, quite suddenly, was full of purpose again.

"But what are we doing this for?" Babs said. "I like to ride with a saddle."

Janet and Billy went on ungirthing their ponies, busy amongst the changing shade.

"Stand up, Octo," Billy said.

"There's no need to take yours off," Janet said at last. "You can keep yours on."

"That's right," said Billy.

"If you're taking yours off," Babs said, "I want to take mine off too."

"You just said you'd like to keep it on."

"I want it off," Babs said. "I want to do what you do."

She was standing under the giant tree with her dress tucked into bloomers and her cherub-face troubled—wide eyes ready for tears and lip going down.

"Then don't argue," Billy said. "We like to ride bare-back, that's all. Here, I'll help you."

"But don't say anything to the Grants," Janet said.

Midget was blowing out her belly, nipping at Babs, thinking the girth was being tightened. Billy lifted his knee and Midget gave in, standing stock-still with her ears back.

"And don't fall off and spoil everything," Billy said, legging Babs on. "Hang on to the mane."

Babs hung on with both hands, kicking her heels into Midget's shoulders. The others kicked air, kicking on, and they were away, galloping heigh! down the white road through the dust to astonish the Grants.

But there was no one outside to see their ride. The children hung about lamely, waiting for the time to leave. Guy brought out his birds' eggs—coloured shells bedded in cotton in boot-box trays—and Janet said nothing about the ostrich egg because they were at the Grants'.

"You've certainly got a lot," Billy said, and Guy put the lids on and put them away carefully on a shelf.

Their father and Mr. Grant came in, talking seriously about Mr. Grant's lighting plant. They sat up straight at tea, and Mrs. Grant asked what they had done with their appetites. At last it was time to go.

Sparrows gossiped among the rose-leaves, and the grown-ups stood under the arch, gossiping too. The children put out shy hands.

"They're certainly growing up," Mr. Grant said.

The children looked at their toes. When the car drove off, they raced for their ponies.

"Don't tell me they're bareback!" Mrs. Grant cried.

Fiercely, like birds released from the hand, they galloped away through the evening, up the hard white road. Janet and Billy were well past the tree before they looked back. The Grants were still watching them from under the arch, Mr. Grant with a leg out to the side and Guy in his white shirt with his leg out at the same angle. Babs had reined away over to where their saddles were stacked behind the gum-tree.

"Come on, Babs!" they called. "Come on!" leaning back over the bouncing rumps of their ponies.

But Babs had dismounted and was struggling with her saddle. The Grants began to walk up the road. Billy and Janet turned their ponies in despair.

"Come on!" they called.

"It's no use," Janet said. "Quick, they mayn't have seen! They think she's in some trouble."

"They may think she's doing something, and stop," Billy said.

Back they galloped to the tree, swinging off their ponies and swinging their saddles on.

"You're mad!" hissed Janet. "Do you want them to

come and catch us?"

"It hurts," Babs said. "It hurts bareback. I bounce."

"Couldn't you wait until they went inside?" Billy hissed.

"I didn't know," Babs said. "Nobody told me."

"Oh, you never know anything."

Babs's face screwed up and tears came out of the cracks like orange-pips.

"I didn't know," she said. "I'm going back to the Grants."

"They're nearly here," Janet whispered. "Oh, come on, Babs."

"I didn't know!" Babs bawled.

"All right. It's all right, Babs. On you get."

And off they galloped.

But next Sunday, when the Grants came over, they played all afternoon with Guy's biplane, running up and down the lawn, making the propellor spin. And Guy said nothing about the saddles.

Descent of a Dove

I

Before the christening, everyone seemed more concerned about the Marshalls and whether they would arrive in time than with Bob and Elsie, who had had the baby. Even while they were arranging the chairs in rows on the lawn under the orange-tree, Mrs. Dalrymple kept saying, "I'm so glad the Marshalls are coming. Frosty wouldn't miss it for the world."

It was strange to hear them called the Marshalls, for the governess and overseer had only been married two weeks before. They had driven off in a brand-new car, with one of Billy's old boots skipping behind, on a honeymoon with Marshall's relations in the north. But they would be back for the christening, for Mr. Marshall was one of the godfathers. The other was Sol Jones.

"I think we'll have the table here, Sol," Mrs. Dalrymple said. "I do hope they're on time."

And she spread a white cloth over the table and arranged a vase of daffodils in one corner.

"Very fetching," Sol said, smoothing the cloth with his blackened hands. "Parson won't know what's hit him."

"But the font!" said Janet. "What are we going to do for a font?"

Their mother's hands paused amongst the daffodils, and Billy said quickly so as not to be done out of his joke, "What about the bird-bath?"

"The very thing!"

Mrs. Dalrymple's fair face lit with pleasure, and she bent down and kissed her clever son.

"The very thing! I'd thought of a china hand-basin, but the bird-bath is made for it."

"But, mum," said Janet, frowning at Billy, "a bird-bath!"

"Don't you worry, Janet," Mrs. Dalrymple said with conviction, "I'm sure God wouldn't mind. In fact" —and her brown eyes lightened—"I couldn't think of anything more appropriate. I've always thought of the Spirit as a bird."

So it was decided on, and Billy, delighted, helped Sol carry the heavy stone pedestal with its flat crowning bowl across the lawn.

"Easy does it!" cried Sol. "You've shipped the whole troughful down the front of my strides."

"I didn't do it," said Billy, for indeed Sol seemed to be staggering more than was necessary.

"Wouldn't like to be this baby," he said. "Bit early yet for duckings. Well, I expect I'd best get into something dry."

"No, no!" cried Mrs. Dalrymple. "You've been to your room quite enough, Sol. No more for today. Remember you're a godfather ... And do stop complaining, Janet. God's far easier to please than some people. Remember Jesus was born in a manger ... Oh dear, look at the time. The Marshalls will be here. I must go and change."

"So must I," said Sol as soon as the wire door banged.

"You may think you're smart," said Janet darkly, "but wait till the heavens open. Then you'll see."

With a half-smile for Janet's benefit, Billy strolled off up the garden path between the flowering mays to listen for the Marshalls.

II

And after all the worry, the Marshalls were the first to arrive. Watching from the ivy, Billy thought that Frosty was having one of her bad days, for she told Mr. Marshall where to park the car—not nearly so new now under the dust—and to put his hat on straight, in just the voice she used when Janet turned up late for lessons; but when she saw Mrs. Dalrymple coming up the path to meet them, she gave a little cry and ran to her.

"Oh, dear," she said, laughing, "it *is* nice to see you. We've had such a time! But it's nice to be back." And she kissed Mrs. Dalrymple on both cheeks and burst into tears.

"Frosty," said Mrs. Dalrymple warmly, "how good to have you back!" She was touched.

"Oh, I am an old fool." Frosty laughed, blowing into her handkerchief. "We've really had the greatest fun. But seeing you ..." And her face wrinkled once again into tears.

"And Mr. Marhsall," said Mrs. Dalrymple, taking his hand. "No need to ask if you enjoyed yourselves. You both look splendid."

"Bit too much travelling for Lois." Marshall shook his head. "And all new people ..."

"Nothing of the sort, Charles. A most interesting trip."

109

The tears were over. Frosty tucked the wet handkerchief down her front.

But her welcome was so affecting that Mrs. Dalrymple led her away by the arm to pick her some flowers, leaving the men together on the verandah.

"And the country up north ..." Doctor Dalrymple said. "How's it looking?"

"Not so good." Marshall spread his legs, relaxing in his chair. "Not so good at all. Not a patch on here."

"And really, Charles's uncle!" Frosty was saying in the garden. "That's the Bredanbone Marshalls. I wish you could see their garden! Acres of it, all watered by turning the one point. Pip! and there you are ... a hundred fountains! No water problem there. But then Bredanbone's on those rich Bredanbone flats. They're so lucky."

"I'm afraid there isn't a great deal out yet," Mrs. Dalrymple said, snipping. "Violets, primroses, hyacinths, little things mostly. But these daffodils are quite sweet."

"Lovely!" Frosty buried her nose in yellow. "Of course the season here is much later than at Bredanbone ... Oh, there you are, Billy! I was just telling your mother ..." And she told him, too.

But what had happened to their governess? She talked so much. Perhaps, if no one interrupted her, she would run down finally like the clock in the hall. That must be what his mother was doing, for she snipped away in silence, nodding and smiling, but with her little headachy frown between her eyes and her lashes drooped.

"I really think it's time to be getting back," she said. "They'll be arriving."

"But I must tell you. I was telling Charles and his uncle ..."

So by the time they got through the orchard and its flowering trees, nearly everybody was gathered on the verandah, the men holding their hats against their blue suits as if afraid of losing them, the women gossiping more easily round the pram.

It was the old pram they all had been wheeled in, but done up like new in a new coat of lacquer; and when she saw it and Elsie standing dumb in the group of women, Mrs. Dalrymple began to run, burdened by the basketful of flowers and holding onto her new straw hat with the other hand.

"Oh, Elsie," she cried, "I'm so sorry! I don't know what could have happened to the time. My goodness, hasn't Dorothy grown! But Kevin's my favourite—and looking his very best for his christening, and just like his father!"

Bob by the wall blushed at his boots, and Elsie said proudly, "And an appetite just like him too. I can hardly keep it up to him."

"Put her on the lucerne flats, Bob," called Sol, and there were cries of "Easy!" and suppressed laughter. Mrs. Dalrymple moved away to greet the others. Frosty took one-year-old Dorothy from the pram.

"This is the little thing *I* want to see," she said. "Ooh, we are fair! We must get that from our mother."

"Put her back," said Elsie.

During the uneasy chatter that followed, Mrs. Marshall could be heard saying to her husband, "Charles, has anyone heard of Mr. Blake since he left so hurriedly? Nearly two years ago, it must be. How time flies!"

"Oh, and Elsie," Mrs. Dalrymple said, turning, "I almost forgot. I picked these flowers for you."

111

And she took the sheaf of daffodils from her basket and laid them down in the broad pram between the two babies.

"There, that must be Mr. Smythe."

The coughing of the parson's car sounded from among the elms.

III

What Billy remembered most about the service was his mother in her flowered hat standing by Mr. Marshall under the orange-tree. Mr. Smythe droned like a winter bee, lifting his eyes to the sky and lowering them to the prayer-book. Elsie, round as the tree, stood by the bird-bath, the baby and sheaf of daffodils caught up in her arms. She kept looking up at Bob and back at the women, a little smile of scorn and triumph on her lips. Sol balanced to the left of Marshall.

Janet kept catching Billy's eye and looking at Sol, and Billy had to think very hard about God to stop himself from laughing. There were the flies he had slammed in his father's ledger, the horns he had snipped from the snail with his mother's mending scissors. But when Mr. Smythe asked if they renounced the pomp and glory of this world and Sol replied in a voice of thick conviction, "I renounce them all!" it was too much for him. The laughter, corked at his mouth, snorted out his nose; and he was alone with pink ears. But his mother turned and smiled with such encouragement that the laughter left him; and he was able to unbutton his coat and keep his eye on the bird-bath just in case the dove came down.

When his mother read that part, sitting on the lawn

or round the fire on Sundays, Billy always thought of the Jordan as just like their own creek, flowing over its sharp sand under the willows; and he saw the sand-pipers, and Jesus wading up to his knees, and the clouds coming over Bald Hill and the dove descending. And the voice of God was like his father's voice talking long-distance on the telephone at night. "That you, George? God here."

But nothing much happened today. Mr. Smythe scooped some water from the bird-bath and spilt it on Kevin's head and made the sign of the cross on Kevin's forehead. And, instead of crying, Kevin opened his mouth and looked about, showing all his gummy jaws. Perhaps that was the miracle, for there was a murmuring amongst the women; and Elsie seemed to think it was, anyway, because she beamed and nodded and kept kissing Kevin when he was given back to her.

"That'll show that old tart Miss Frost," she said afterwards.

But when it was all over, Mr. Smythe kept them there getting cold while he took the opportunity. He wanted to thank the Dalrymples, for he always liked ... There were some new faces ... And he hoped ... And he went on to talk about miracles, his earnest, shortsighted gaze searching the misting orchard as if God walked there somewhere, plain to be seen, if only his eyes were better. But what he said was different. He said that miracles had a perfectly down-to-earth, scientific explanation if only they were looked at steadily with clear eyes. For example, the descent of the dove at Christ's baptism was nothing but a metaphorical turn of phrase. The dove did not descend. What was important was the meaning behind the words, the descent of the Spirit. We must live in our century.

Billy looked sideways at Janet, because, if there were no dove, perhaps Jesus hadn't stood in their creek with the clouds coming over. But Janet was shifting about in her chair like everyone else, and their father coughed more loudly, and Mr. Smythe, dropping his eyes from the shadowy garden, gathered up his books.

"But perhaps we need more time," he said. "The service is over."

Their father rose.

"Very interesting," he said. "There was the changing of the water into wine. I've always thought ..." And he led Mr. Smythe away towards the verandah where the decanter stood amongst glasses.

The women gathered round Kevin.

"Don't know about you," Sol said, "but there's grog on. My tongue's like a lizard."

IV

After nearly everyone had gone—Elsie smiling and blushing, saying, "Oh-ho, don't you believe it! He's not always like that!" and Bob thanking his toes, and Sol protesting, "But, by the living Lord, I must shift them chairs in before lights-out!"—they stood around, exhausted and smiling, except Frosty who wanted to tell Doctor Dalrymple about her trip.

"A hundred sprinklers," she said, "like little fairy fountains! I wish you could see them."

"I don't know about the fairies, but I can see the expense."

"I was wondering," Marshall said on the side, "if you might have a few bulbs for our garden?"

"Come along!" cried Mrs. Dalrymple. "There's still

114

light enough. I'll dig you some."

But Frosty was too absorbed to see them go, talking of Bredanbone and the Country Women's.

"That's what we need here," she said. "A really strong branch. We're too taken up with flower shows. Now, if I had my way ... but Charles won't push, he has no spirit."

Dalrymple did not seem to be listening, his eyes lost in darkness beyond the ghostly trees. From the garden came the rise and fall of voices, the cry of a bird.

"Well, well," he said, turning wearily, "so there was no dove after all."

"No dove? Oh, yes, I quite agree. We've got to be practical these days."

And then she noticed, too, that the others had gone, and for a time was silent. But not for long.

"Whatever could have happened to Charles?" she cried. "We should have been home hours ago. There are my new hens. But it's just like him."

And she began calling, "Charles! Charles!" her voice rising and rising in the misty evening amongst the owls.

"Charles, at once!"

"Coming!"

Laughing, Marshall and Mrs. Dalrymple came up the path.

"No, no," she was saying. "you most certainly do not chop the tops off. You let the good soak back into the bulb, and they fall off."

"Charles!" cried Frosty. "I've been so worried. It's late. You're so inconsiderate."

"But, Lois, we've been digging—"

"Nonsense," she said harshly. "You don't care a rap for flowers."

It was a hurried departure.

Mrs. Dalrymple said she hoped they'd be comfortable in their new cottage, and if there was anything ... And Frosty thanked her and said she expected that she'd manage.

"At all events, come over soon to lunch," called Mrs. Dalrymple after the dusty car.

But she was crestfallen and agitated until her husband took her arm and walked her slowly down the path towards the square lights of the house.

"She won't come," he said. "That's a certainty." And he sighed. "But what I am pleased about is Bob and Elsie. I think I may say I had a hand in that."

"Oh, Andrew!" His wife laughed. "You don't think I encouraged the other?"

"Well, perhaps not," said Dalrymple, smiling and pressing her arm. "I think, though, I might allow myself another whisky tonight. Sherry for you?"

And he was right, the Marshalls came seldom. Sometimes the children walked over, but Frosty talked so much that Janet was sick in the creek coming home. So they visited Elsie more often instead. The only way Billy could ever explain the difference between them was that the dove had descended on the one and not on the other.

Other Stories

... *the act of the hawk, which she watched, hawk-like, was a moment of shrill beauty that rose above the endlessness of bone. The red eye spoke of worlds that were brief and fierce.*

Patrick White
The Aunt's Story

Tom Death

Jim Gray and Harvey Lockyer kept a skeleton in a cupboard. The cupboard had a rope handle on either side and every Friday night they carried it from their quarters to the mess to shout the skeleton a glass of beer. The name of the skeleton was Tom Death.

The mess was a long timbered barnroom on a wooded rise. Fence-posts blazed in the fireplaces at opposite ends, the flames licking through the adzed rail-holes and burning a welcome in the frosty panes. Aircrew stood in groups along the long bar, drinking and talking shop.

"Gangway!" Harvey Lockyer would cry. "Gangway for Tom Death!"

They would hoist the cupboard up onto the corner of the bar and throw the doors wide. Inside, on a high stool, sat the skeleton with its legs crossed. It gazed from hollow sockets over the heads of the laughing men.

"How's Tom tonight?" a friend would ask. "Beer, Jim? Harvey?"

When the beers came, Gray would raise his eyebrows.

"Here, here!" he would say. "Where are your manners? You're one light. Aren't you going to buy a beer for Tom? Gets pretty dry shut up in a cupboard all day."

"Corporal! A beer for Tom!"

And Harvey Lockyer smiling seriously and scolding the skeleton for spilling the beer, would tilt back the creaking head and tilt the glass. Much of the beer was spilled, for Lockyer took a generous delight in watching his friend Gray.

Jim Gray was a fair, sharp-boned, handsome young man of nervous wit. He had fitted the skeleton out with a stomach of glass tubes that ended in a retort; and while the amber column wound slowly down the thin spiral, Gray gesticulated with laughter.

"God! look at him!" he would cry, his fine face lit up in the firelight and his eyes widely blue. "What a life, eh!" crowding the others around the cupboard. "What a life! Free beer and no dawn take-offs."

And slapping the skeleton on its bony, wire-jointed knee, he would say, "You fell on your feet all right, Tom. You know what's good for you."

"And who empties the retort?"

There was much coming and going on the station, new crews arriving each month for war training and trained crews leaving for advance squadrons in the north. And one of the newcomers unused to the tension in the Valley, to the gusty infection of Gray's laughter, would ask the question with a knowing smile, a smile that faltered before the lean symbol in the cupboard.

"And who drinks Death's share? "

"Now now," Jim Gray would say. "No coarseness in front of Tom, Tom."

The newcomer would perhaps explain that his own name was not Tom; but after a week in the Valley he would know differently. Everyone, including the skeleton, was Tom. Tom had become the general term of address.

It was used mainly for convenience; for no one could keep up with all the names. But there were other reasons.

The training course was a tough one and the lean twin-engined bombers were difficult to fly and unreliable. Many crashed—too many. It made men nervous, and crews leaving for the war sang songs and sometimes broke the furniture in the mess. An explanation had to be found for the high death rate, and the theorists found it.

It was, they said, simply a matter of economics. In the south there was a reserve of aircraft; up north, every aircraft was needed. Consequently, the bad pilots were weeded out during training.

The flying instructors saw the point and took care. They called their pupils Tom and were spared any heartaches over Dick and Harry. Life was kept at arm's length but Death drank intimately with them in his open cupboard.

As the Friday evenings wore towards morning, a wild gay look would come into Harvey Lockyer's shy eyes, for three friends had been shot from his wingtip in the islands; and he would sing, swaying in friendly chorus:

"I'm going to a better land where everything is
    right,
Where whisky grows on the coconut trees and you
    go home every night;
Where there's nothing else to do all day but sit
    around and sing;
C'est beaucoup and women too! Oh, Death,
    where is your sting?"

Gray laughed but drank little; and when no one was left for Lockyer to sing with, Gray led him to their cold quarters and went back for Tom Death.

The next morning if they were not flying, they drank the beer in the retort; and Lockyer returning to the bar would complain in his quiet dry way that someone had dug a hole outside the door of the mess and that he had fallen into it on going to bed.

"It's not the digging of the hole that I mind," he would explain. "It's the way its filled in the next morning as though it had never been there. Shows lack of moral fibre to my mind; and besides, someone might get buried."

Jim Gray would double up with laughter.

It was mid-winter in the Valley when Gray was late for his Friday night appointment. They carried the cupboard to the mess as usual and there Gray went through elaborate farewells.

"Got to fly," he said, crossing himself. "Mine's a double brandy. Neat, thanks Corporal."

He fed the brandy to Tom Death, throwing back his head to laugh, and took Harvey Lockyer by the hand.

"Goodbye, old boy," he said. "It's been a good life."

"Nice to have known you," said Lockyer. "But I don't like brandy in the morning."

The fires crumbled in a rose glow and the men smiled at the bar.

"Don't fly too high or too fast," someone warned.

Gray raised an acknowledging finger, shook hands with the skeleton; he winked an eye, gripping the dead bone.

"See you later," he said.

As he walked out of the mess, the wind fumbled at the locks of the windows. It waited around the corner with a knife. It was a cold night, sharp with frost, with stars.

—No fogs, anyway, Gray thought, feeling his great-coat lap about him down the rise. Below, the shallow valley cupped the lights for warmth, green and white and crimson; and around the perimeter of the airstrip gaunt hands of trees reached up into the star-shine. He was stinging-warm by the time he came to the farmhouse.

A roar of engines running up, dust blowing through the orchard, lean metal shapes caught in a web of boughs, men green and drowned beneath the glow of wing-lights, the glare of a page—an aerodrome is vivid in the night. Jim Gray climbed into the right-hand seat and checking the oil temperature, adjusting his throat microphone, said, "Take her away!" The aircraft rolled through darkness to the taxying stand.

—He'll be the next, Gray thought, looking sideways in the dim lighting at the big sure-jawed, sure-handed, raven man whom he had to train. He said aloud, "You can sit her down prettily enough, Tom; but these kites take care. Have you forgotten anything?"

The big man smiled. Gray noticed the excessive whiteness and evenness of his teeth and that the top and bottom teeth met like the tipping of fingers.

"Bob's the name", he said. "Bob Sutherland. No, I don't think I've forgotten anything."

He blinked the navigation lights and was given a green by the control officer. A quarter way down the flarepath when the engines burnt red under the cowls and power shook the aircraft, Gray said, "Doesn't feel right, does it? Taking over."

With surprising quickness he slapped down the flap lever, wound the trim-tab, checked the flaps. The aircraft climbed steadily into the night.

Gray lifted the flaps, reduced power.

"See what I mean?" he said. "You take off with fifteen per cent flap—Tom".

Sutherland smiled his vivid smile.

"Right," he said.

They turned in to land. As the wheels came down, the nose tilted and Gray said, "Notice anything?"

Sutherland studied the lighted panel and said slowly, "The instruments show that one wheel's only half down".

"What are you going to do about it?"

A snarling twisted expression came into Sutherland's face and he said, "Look here Gray. Is this another of your tricks?"

"I wish it were, Tom," Gray said, meeting the big man with half-humorous eyes. "What are you going to do about it?"

They crossed the smoking flares on full power. Throttling back, Sutherland raised and lowered the undercarriage several times, watching the instruments. "I'll carry out emergency procedure," he said.

"First, Tom, we'll make a visual check; and then we'll climb to seven thousand feet".

The aerodrome receded to pinpoints of lights.

At altitude, the night was smooth and cold, clustered with navigable stars. The torn air screamed in the cowlings, sucked at the window-glass. A knife of moon rose in the west.

"Back—back," Gray was saying, watching the speed sink until the aircraft trembled. "Now—forward! —Back! Forward!"

The manual emergency devices had failed to lower the undercarriage. Now he was teaching Sutherland to shake the wheels down. Sutherland's left leg danced three times on the rudder pedal.

"All right," Gray said. "I'll take over. Have a cigarette."

The other drew the good smoke deep down into his lungs, and Gray said, "You'll be right now, Bob. You can fly this aircraft as well as I can; but you're careless. You've got to be careful in these kites. You live longer."

Sutherland raised his eyes and smiled, regarded the point of his cigarette.

"All right," he said. "It was the cold.—You're a good fellow, Gray.—But how do we get down out of this?"

"I'll have a go at shaking 'em down," Gray said. "And after all—belly-landings aren't as bad as that." Then laughing his infectious nervous laugh, he said, "I'll beg Harvey Lockyer is as blind as a bat by this time. You'll have to join us, Bob."

Looking down he tried to pick out the mess among the Pleiades cluster of the lights.

Back, back.—Forward!—Back! Forward!

Gray rocked the aircraft, keeping the speed slightly above the stall. Until the moment that he took over, he had been enjoying himself. He had watched the big man wrestle the aircraft, used to getting his own way. He saw the exasperation in his eyes, the sweat prick through his forehead in the cold; watching idly like a cat until Sutherland glanced sideways showing the whites of his eyes, until his foot trembled involuntarily at the controls. And then he knew that Sutherland would live; that he could teach him to fly. Up to that point it had been just a very good lesson.

Now it was his job to get the wheels down.

And there was the darkness—darkness between the stars, darkness between the lights—a darkness that was one. And there was a dim panel of instruments to tell him where the earth was. The aircraft shook at the stall, plunged, rose, plunged. Flying was Gray's business.

"That's one wheel well and truly down," he said. "I've shifted the other a little. Check that hydraulic oil tank again. All gone? I thought so. Look, do you mind having a leak in it? That sometimes works."

For three-quarters of an hour he rocked the aircraft, climbing at intervals to make up for lost altitude.

"Time for a cigarette," he said. "One thing, it keeps you warm."

He had opened the collar of his greatcoat and was circling down slowly towards the lights.

"No go?" Sutherland asked.

"No."

Gray worked the undercarriage lever up and down. "You've noticed?" he said. "The other leg is stuck in the down position."

"Not so good."

"That's what I mean," Gray said. "I think it would be best if you baled out."

"What about you?"

"This is my pigeon," Gray said with a grimace. "I'll land her. But it might be best for you …"

"I'll stay," Sutherland said. And meeting Gray's cold humorous eyes, he smiled, joining white teeth. "Oh, you needn't worry about that! I'm no little Briton. On the contrary. There's something solid under you here. While out there … " He spread a hand to the night. "Have you ever baled out?"

"No," Gray said. "But I would—in your position."

"I think you'll get away with it."

Sutherland had set his jaw.

"Well, two's company."

And suddenly Gray laughed his doubling-up

laughter, resting a hand on Sutherland's shoulder. "There's no doubt about it!" he said. "You're a stubborn bastard. You're as bad as Lockyer. It'll get you into trouble one day. By the way, you didn't bring any cards did you? We've got three hours ahead of us, running the petrol out. Dumping's a trap in these kites."

The aircraft circled above the smoking gold, the stone green, and warm crimson, of the lights in the Valley.

The watchers saw the navigation lights move between the stars.

"That's Jupiter," one said. "Jupiter's out tonight. There's Betelguese—the hot red star."

"And there," said another, "is Jim Gray."

They all laughed, standing in groups among the dark fruit trees, waiting. The medical officer checked through his gear.

"Keep the motor warmed up," he told the driver of the ambulance.

There was no one at the bar but Tom Death in his open cupboard.

That night, without Jim Gray to crowd them around, the skelton had been almost a failure. The men talked of other things, took their drinks to the fire. And Lockyer, surprisingly sober, realized that it was not the skeleton at all, but his friend's laughter, that gave the edge to life, making the evenings short and gay. The skeleton took second place.

Then the news came that an aircraft was in trouble.

"Who is it this time? Not Jim!"

The wind chafed in the boughs of the fruit trees.

"Sutherland's with him. He won't be missed."

"I never did like that big bastard," Lockyer said.

The night hid the anger and pain in his eyes. He was

convinced that Sutherland had got Gray into this. Someone was to blame.

—There's something fatal about me, he thought, standing in the cold blast and watching the endless circling of the navigation lights.

"Flight Lieutenant Lockyer!" A voice was calling through the orchard.

"Seen Harvey about? Oh, there you are. You're wanted at the control tower."

He climbed the steep ladder into the night. Below the lighted box, the flares rocked in the wind like buoys on a harbour.

"Oh, Harvey, Gray wants a word with you."

Lockyer slipped on the head set, took up the microphone.

"That you Jim?" he said. "What's it like up there?"

"Cold," Gray's voice came back. "Lot of stars about. How's the party going?"

"Fine," Lockyer said. "Better hurry up. Tom's had your share so far. Getting pretty groggy."

He heard Gray's involuntary laughter.

"All right, old boy. Just wanted to know how things are going. Gets lonely up here. Shout Tom one for me."

"All right," Lockyer said. "See you later."

He was thoughtful as he laid down the microphone.

"Anything up?" the control officer asked. He was a heavy greying man who did not fly.

"Oh no," Lockyer said twisting a smile. "Just wanted to know how the party's going."

The control officer was still chuckling as Lockyer climbed down from the tower.

A few new arrivals had returned to the mess, tired of waiting, and were warming their backs at the fire.

Lockyer was suddenly embarrassed.

"Pretty cold," he said, rubbing his hands above the veined coals. "Feel like a drink?"

"Not just now, thanks."

There was a pause and Lockyer said, "Think I will. Need something to keep you warm!"

"Yes, it's cold," he said a moment later. "If you won't, I expect Tom will drink with me."

He went to the bar and ordered two beers. He drank half his own and carried the other to the cupboard, conscious of the officers watching him.

"Here you are Tom," he said. "Feeling thirsty?"

Almost brutally he jerked back the skeleton's head. And as the slim column of beer wound through the tubes, he did not feel like laughing at all.

Outside, above the rattling of the wind at the latches, he could hear the beat of engines. The sound slowly faded as the aircraft moved towards the distant edge of its circuit.

Gray landed on one wheel, holding the wing up with stick and rudder and a tension of wind, until the tip pitched, ploughing into the clay. The aircraft spun like an exhausted top and came to rest.

"That's three pounds fifteen you owe me, Bob," Gray said, in the white glare of the headlights.

But in the utility driving to the mess, he thrust his face out into the clean dark air and laughed silently, in agony, for several minutes.

The next week there was a mock parade and the skeleton was presented in his cupboard to the station hospital with full military honours.

"Guard! Reverse arms!"

The Knife

I

"All right," the flat voice said in his ear. "She's all yours."

"Taking over," Max Viner said.

There were five aircraft ahead: two on the cross-wind leg, three on the approach. The runway was hidden under the port wing—just the way he liked it.

"I'll take her in," he said.

And, as they had to in the jungle, he acted very quickly: chopped back the throttle, dropped the port wing, trod on the upper rudder. And while the aircraft fell away, he felt the stick into the right-hand corner, feeling with his fingers for the stall, learning as he went, his head to the side watching the strip over his shoulder, the instruments forgotten. The earth was coming up at him sideways with a rush of air; and just where the controls softened, he held them, stick and rudder; dropped the wheels, the flaps, letting the nose come round until the end of the runway was there, where he wanted it, coming like a train in the angle of the wing and engine. Almost at the point of impact, he changed rudder pedals. The nose came up and round sweetly into the line of flight. He kicked three times each way washing out the last of the speed, the stick in his guts. When the aircraft stalled, the runway took the

130

three points cleanly with no feeling of touch-down at all—a slight shudder, an easing of the olios.

He turned off the strip a third of the way down. The other aircraft were still way up: three on the approach, two on the cross-wind leg—not like the boys of the squadron who would be there, swinging in beside him, lifting their thumbs.

"She's sweet," he said. "She's a sweet kite for a trainer. Thanks a lot. I know her now."

"If you'll taxi back," the voice was saying, "we'll do a normal circuit and landing."

"Just as you like."

But when he went for a burst of throttle, the lever was held back, dead.

"Look both ways," the voice said. "Then take her around on an even throttle by the taxiing lane."

Viner loosened the safety-strap, turned around, his elbow on the fuselage, and smiled at the man in the cockpit behind him. He met two candid eyes above the mouthpiece.

"Can't we skip that," he said. "I know all the patter. Let's just brush up at the bar, huh?"

"You're not on operations now," the voice said in his ear. "Teach that landing to your pupils and we'd have no aircraft left at the end of a week."

"Jolly good, eh? We'd all get some leave.—But seriously, that may have been a bit smart. I know how it goes though: wheels, 1,500; flaps on the turn. Watch the instruments and kiss my aunt. It doesn't work like that in practice."

"We'll try it," the voice said. The straight eyes had not smiled.

All right, he'd try it, if that was the way of it. Knee deep in tape. And from a man who'd not seen a shot fired in anger!

All the way around the voice was in his ear. Stealthily he disconnected the inter-com. cord. He was free at last to breathe, to look out at the great hot hemisphere of sky: mountains in the distance and no threat in the sun. A friendly corner where a man could relax, forget the tension in his hand. But the tension was there, he felt it, the old anger, the wariness—this time for the man in the seat behind him, the man with the cold voice and the soft job.

If it was kid-stuff he wanted, Viner would give it to him: the standard circuit, the groove cut in the sky back home above Forrest Hill, two tours ago. He could do it with his eyes shut. And again he felt the prickle of his moustache as he smiled, in the old groove, following the leader onto the broad arm of the runway crossing the plain.

He swept in on the merry-go-round with a trickle of throttle, ready to wheel her on. But for some reason he was uncomfortable; there was too much time. He checked late. The port wheel struck first and the earth threw them at the sky, nose high and a wing going over. A burst of motor to ease her—but the aircraft was no longer his. The throttle moved in his hand, and the stick. The instructor had taken over.

Furious, he switched on the inter-com., and maddeningly the cold voice proceeded "the wheels and then the flaps at 500 feet, easing back the throttle."

"Here!" Viner said. "What do you mean, taking over? Who's flying this crate?"

"I am," the voice said, "—Squadron Leader Viner. Take her around again, and this time, check earlier. Bring the tail down in stages. And by the way, leave the microphone on. Handing over."

"All right—Squadron Leader Evans," Viner said. "Taking over."

He was white, dead white with anger; but his eyes—his shrewd, brown, calculating eyes that knew so well the angles through the gunsights, just where to freeze and for how long, while the tracer ripped, it seemed, from them studding the enemy craft, each kill a mathematical ecstacy, a thing of the mind—these eyes were shrewd again, calm.

They spent the morning there, practising circuits and bumps.

"Well, that's all right," Dad Evans said, climbing out, swinging off his sweating helmet, rubbing a hand through greying hair. The tar sweated. Wingtip to wingtip, the training two-seaters shimmered in line down the plain. The last aircraft coughed, shutting off. Hawks wheeled again in the fierce sky. Brown-skinned pupils trailed out of the hangars for lunch.

"That's all right. You settled down well after the first round or two. It's strange, I guess, after operations. They all find it. Here it's a matter of saving lives—through care."

Max Viner smiled. He rubbed his moustache down, checking the smile. He looked about him, the smile still itching at his moustache—at the brown-skinned trainees and the hawks in the sky.

"Squadron Leader Evans," he said. "May I see you in your office. Officially."

"Certainly." Evans met his eyes. "I'll be there after lunch. And if it's official, shall we make it two o'clock?"

He was smiling.

"Two o'clock."

Viner swung the parachute onto his shoulder and brushing down his moustache, walked off into the hangar.

At two o'clock he saluted and said,

"Sir, I would like to make a formal application—I believe that's the phrase ... "

"Cut it," Evans said. "Sit down."

But Viner did not sit down. Instead, he leaned his hands on the desk so that the fingers whitened.

"Sir, I'd like to return to my squadron."

"Sit down. Don't be a fool."

"But you see, I am not a fool. I want to return to operations."

"You've done your two tours," Evans said. "You need a rest. Look at you."

"What's wrong with me?" Fire suddenly shot in Viner's eyes. "Look at that hand." It was his trigger hand, hard, steady. "You think because of this morning ... "

"I think nothing of the sort. It's usual, after operations. Relax. You've done with the war."

"So you won't recommend it?"

And quite suddenly Viner did relax. He put his hands in his pockets. He sauntered stiff-kneed over the linoleum.

"Well well," he said. "Just so long as we know. It's a pleasure to learn. So it's circuits and bumps. Training boongs."

"That's another thing," Evans said, "while we're getting to know one another. There are no boongs on this station. Remember that. There are ourselves, and our allies."

Viner stood still. He looked at the other. He raised his eyebrows. He smiled—a little partisan smile.

"That's good," he said. "That's good. Where did you get that one? Ourselves—and our allies!" He had loosened a button of his jacket and slipped his hand in against his hammering heart. "Say that often enough and maybe—there's always the chance—maybe you'll get that O.B.E. after all."

He was smiling his most charming smile, a smile that made him young again, reckless and arrogant.

"Squadron Leader Viner," Evans said. He was tapping the desk with a pencil, tired now, a little old. "I thought we might talk things out. You came here with a good record—I almost said brilliant. It would be a pity to spoil it. You will take over 'A' Flight tomorrow. Right?"

"Right, sir."

All the way over to the mess, Viner kept repeating, "Ourselves—and our allies!" The imperturbability of Evans infuriated him—that grave pipe-smoker's smile: like Christmas pudding; like Dr. Mac. Somehow it seemed to him theatrical; but he admitted envy; he who was most composed, most at ease, at 500 m.p.h. with the enemy in his sights.

And at the bar he found suddenly that he was shaking, trembling all over, in a fever, like his spells at night when he woke shaken by unknown terrors.

"You all right, sir?"

"Of course I'm all right. Whisky and soda, Corporal."

To prove it, he lifted the drink, his hand firm again, unflinching, and toasted the bar-steward.

"To ourselves," he said. "And our allies!"

There was nobody else in the mess.

And after the third whisky, the cold fire, he could smile again, easily; smile the slow arrogant smile that he pushed down, thumbing his moustache.

"Yes," he said, "Corporal. We're going to see a lot of one another. See this corner?"

"Yes, sir,"

"You'll find me here."

He took a knife from his pocket, opened the blade, and cut a quadrant on the bar counter between the wall and his elbow. His reserve. Then he dug the knife in the soft wood of the bar with the cutting edge to the world. It was war.

II

He was there each evening and night, leaving his corner only for dinner. The corporal had his whisky and soda ready for him when he came in from flying and he drank steadily until midnight. But he did not get drunk. The only change as the evenings wore on, was the little smile that lifted the corners of his moustache. He would thumb it down but it would return, though his eyes were cold.

"The same again, Corporal."

He drank at first on his own. Then two or three officers took to drinking with him, those with a grouch, with an itch, the fashionably bored. They tried at first to get him drunk, to out-drink him.

"Step up the pace," they said. "I'll take over from you at eleven."

In the end they fell into his ways.

His end of the bar got the name of C.O.D. It was a Viner, his own joke—the Corner of Discontent. Their toast was, "To ourselves—and our allies!" And they clinked glasses gravely.

Then his flight came over, for he knew how to lead men.

He would look a man hard in the eyes—a pause, a

calculation. And after he would laugh, tease; he was gay and charming. But the look was remembered, like the sear of a knife. Their own weapons sheared off for he did not seek even their company. They came to him.

Deliberately, too, he neglected station orders, overlooked them, let his men do as they liked. Then he enforced them, as he chose, as his own orders—a round turn, the reins suddenly hard. The hand was there: look out! His arrogance, his charm, his dozen kills, did the rest.

"You never quite know," they said, "quite how to take Max."

Gradually the atmosphere on the training station changed. It was evident in the way the officers wore their peaked caps—the crowns tented, creased fore and aft, operational style. There were more accidents, they drank more, there were all-night parties in the mess. But what worried Dad Evans was the feeling between the staff and the trainees—between the white instructors and their dark-skinned pupil-pilots: a subtle change, a lack of trust, a look in the eye. And the grave toast, "to our allies!"

Evans saw it and worried. He suffered in other ways too. He found himself drinking with the older non-flying men. There were hints, silences. He had not flown on operations.

"That forward strip," a boy said. "What-do-you-call-it?—cut out under the mountain? Max says they landed and refuelled ten kites there in thirty minutes—touch-down to take-off. What do they call it? You'd remember.—No, you weren't in Burma."

And the boy looked down, silenced.

Evans felt it keenly. It was the trouble with the trainees, he told himself, that he did not like. But there was nothing tangible. And as a flight commander, Max Viner knew his job.

He put his flight on a war footing.

"They're going to the war, aren't they?" he said, "these allies. That's the idea, isn't it? Well, we'll train them under war conditions."

And he dispersed his aircraft.

He trained his men to get away quickly.

"Right," he said. "There's a raid."

He stood by the window watching them, a microphone in his hand.

His formations took off like clockwork. There was an exact patter, an exact drill. He gave them interceptions, evasive tactics, his voice always with them, sharp as a knife, from the leading aircraft or the transmitter in his office. It was the same when they landed: disperse, refuel.

He worked his instructors as hard as himself, at fever pitch. And at night he showed them how to drink.

"You're late," he said next morning. "We don't have hangovers here. Let's see," and he smiled. "There's a job on tonight, cross-country. Take off at ten and at two. You'll lead both formations. Right?—Hum. You don't look too good. Better take a kite up now and clear your head."

They grumbled and liked it. His ideas caught on. All aircraft were dispersed. The aircraftsmen grumbled and liked it too.

"It's all right," they said, "for Buggerlugs," craning their necks at the ice-chalkings a mile up above the hawks. "He doesn't fry his fanny in this heat. Just feel that leading-edge."

Then the aircraft came down with the sound half a sky behind, and they swung around, talking of Viner.

"It's the moustache that gets me in."

"You've got to hand it to him. He can fly a kite."

And the trainees, though they hated him—hating the bland patronage of his smile, his clipped speech, abrupt as gunfire—responded. This was the real thing. Dad Evans's methods, safety first, were on the way out.

Once a week Viner checked through all the pupils in his flight.

"I don't mind if you kill yourself," he told them. "But don't kill me. Leave that till you're solo."

He finished each test high up above the low-flying area.

"Right-oh," he said. "Taking over."

The aircraft tipped on its wing and went down past the vertical. Air screamed, and quite suddenly the wide plain of paddy fields with its lazy river became one field, a bullock dray, a straw hat. And blacked out in the front cockpit, they knew they were rolling, a confused world of greens and browns rolling round like a barrel. Then they were climbing, stalling, coming down again to roll along the river between the palms.

"Work with me," he said. "That's it. That's it. That's It!"

And they climbed again for a simple roll at three hundred feet, working together, the nose pivoting on the horizon.

"That's the stuff. That's the stuff. You'll make a fighter pilot yet."

But when they landed—his own landing: slip, kick, and wash out speed; once only for each pupil—the old smile was back on his mouth, mocking, superior. And the clipped voice:

"But that's not for you, remember. You've got to be a pilot before you can fly.—If you've got it in you ... "

The same formula for each: the smile and the warning. It drove them wild. It was almost as if he taunted them with his skill, daring them to match it. They would practice rolls high up amongst the vapour trails.

Then towards the end of the course, there was a succession of accidents, three in a week. Dad Evans looked into them. The wreckage told him little: long scars across the paddy fields. An engine three feet in. The aircraft had exploded on impact. All he had as a lead was the place: they had all happened in the low flying area; and the fact that the pilots were pupils in Viner's flight.

But when a fourth went in, he felt the pain of it in his own body. He walked thoughtfully to the mess.

There was no one in the mess but Viner. He was in his usual corner having his first for the day. The low sun threw burning slats from the foot of the blinds.

"Max," he said, "I've got some news for you."

"News?"

Viner no longer masked the contempt in his eyes. He had the station with him. His knife was open on the counter and he spun it, looking down with his black brows raised.

"You know, Max, I'm beginning to wonder a little. Those accidents last week—they were all in your flight."

"They go in threes."

"But this evening there was another."

Viner's eyes became very still.

"Who was it?"

"Another of yours. And in the same way."

"All right," Viner said. "We're not playing Bo Peep. These things happen. What are you drinking—whisky? Or,"—and the old smile was back, twitching his lip. He smoothed it. "Or maybe, Dad, you'd like some champagne."

While the whisky came, he played with the knife, whittling at the counter, lost in thought.

"Things aren't going well for you, Dad," he said, "are they? You don't want to let it influence you. Methods change.—Was that your news?"

"You're fond of that knife," Evans said. "You're fond of whittling, aren't you Max?"

On an impulse he leaned forward and ran his finger along the counter edge. Three serrations bit into his flesh—the beginnings of a fourth. It was all he needed. He straightened up.

"No," he said, "Viner. This is my news. You're grounded. I'm sending you home."

And he held Viner's wrist while they looked into each other's eyes.

But for some reason when Viner left, Evans took to drinking on his own. He went missing soon after on operations over Burma.

Tumult in the Clouds

I

The Coral-pink Elephant

On an island airstrip, two young men met face to face behind the mole of a bofors-gun emplacement. It was fifteen minutes before take-off. In jungle green, mae-wests, and silk-map cravats, they eyed one another obliquely, with mild surprise and sympathetic calculation.

A thin bush of bent gum trees flanked the strip, and they chose separate saplings to stand behind.

"I see," said Joss Brown, "that you have all your trophies up, Havelock."

Ellis, a short, curly headed young man, blushed behind his tree and felt for the toy koala bear hanging from his neck on a length of fishing line. He felt a fool. He liked to believe that his animal mascots were invisible to everyone but himself. And he discouraged comment.

"If I like to wear them," he said, "that's my business."

He thrust a short defiant jaw around the gum trunk but was surprised by the understanding in the other's eyes.

142

"Do they bring you luck, Havelock?" Brown asked.

"Well, they do and they don't," said Ellis. "That is, I'm not sure. I never fly without them."

Brown stroked a long under-slung jaw that he usually wore forward, and said:

"Do you wear them for association's sake, then?"

Ellis brought his black brows together and fumbled cautiously at his shirt-front for his coral-pink elephant.

"Not exactly," he said. "Though I expect I did in the first place."

Brown came out from behind his tree into the raw sunlight and said outright:

"Then what the devil do you wear them for?"

This approach frightened Ellis. He sidled behind his tree and gazed up through wide boughs at the unanswering sky.

"I like to wear them," he said. "That's good enough reason for me; and it'll have to be good enough for you."

But Brown had seated himself on a fallen branch and was running his hand through his short red hair in the attitude of a thinker.

"I'm not meaning to be rude," he said. "I expect we all have our fears and superstitions. Forget it."

This brought Ellis out from behind his tree.

"Well, there's no great secret about it really," he said. "They've just become a sort of habit. I wore them on my first solo and got away with that all right. It's just that I wouldn't feel comfortable without them now. I expect it's bloody silly, really."

He looked at Brown and Brown did not seem to think so. He was sitting on the fallen branch, running his hand through his hair.

"In fact ... " Ellis said. He changed his mind, said,

143

"'Bout time we were starting up;" and hurried away around the mole, the elephant hanging a little less heavily about his neck.

Brown watched him go, squat and young and thoughtful; but he did not follow. He sat still in the hard sunlight, thinking.

He was thinking that if he could see Ellis clearly enough, he might be able to see himself too.

He knew Ellis's father, a grey, hand-smoothing chemist on the corner of the high street at home.

If his son lived, he too would weigh out drugs in that soap-smelling shop.

In the meantime, Ellis knew with fatal certainty that should he lose one of his stuffed toys, sudden death would meet him in the centre of a shell-burst.

Brown stood up and kicked with blunt boots at the knots of grass.

And here was he, an affable young stock-broker, about to set out on a dangerous mission. Did he sweat at the thought of death from shell-fire? Not a bit. He had a transcending fear of night flying.

He dreaded the horizonless night and the final turn into wind when the flare-path squares out and becomes a dangerous oasis in a desert of black air. The road to the normal world lies dim and narrow under the nose; and on either side, in darkness, huddle the malicious trees.

And yet, six weeks ago, night flying had been easy; it had been no trouble at all.

Brown was brought back to daylight by the cough of a motor. The formation was starting up. He stood there, thinking that if only he had time, an hour, a minute he would see things in perspective and conquer this unreasonable fear.

Another motor coughed. There wasn't the time.

Brown stamped the good earth beneath his feet; said, "Be good to me, pal;" and walked resolutely around the mole to his aircraft.

He noticed that the shadow of the aircraft lay across the strip.

II

One More Turn Round

A Catalina flying-boat circled a map position above a dull sea. The sea was stirred by currents that faded out in hazy distances. The two pilots were throwing dice.

They had the automatic-pilot in control and they threw the dice on a pasteboard map between the seats.

"Financially, this is the most successful operation I've been on for some time," Joe Read said. "Pity we have to go home."

He was extremely small, bolstered up and forward on cushions in the captain's seat. His hand as he smoothed the curves of his rust-red moustache, was like the hand of a child reaching up to find out whether the moustache was real.

"One more circuit, Joe; one more turn round," Scott said. "Your luck can't last at this pace."

"Well, if you want to throw your money down the drain ... "

And he was crooning endearments to the dice as if they were little women when his wireless operator called him on the inter-communication gear.

"Skip, an emergency distress signal is just coming

145

through; relayed from Darwin."

"All right, all right."

Read threw the dice, collected the stake, and banking the flying-boat over on its wing, commenced to climb north-west into the setting sun.

"Probably the other bloody way," he said. "It always is. Let's have the message as soon as you've decoded it. How about some coffee, Mac?"

As the flying-boat gained height, he could see the mountains on the horizon, and the cloud towering above the mountains, like blue rock. The Catalina climbed at eighty-five knots.

"Here's the message, Skip," the operator said. "Six men afloat in a dinghy one mile north of the target. One Mitchell top cover. How do you like that?"

"God blast their eyes," said Read. "Why the devil didn't we hear of this before? The strike's been over for three quarters of an hour at least."

"There's probably a skip distance," the operator said, "and they couldn't contact us. This wireless is behaving like a bag-full of cats."

"Then drown 'em," said Read.

At seven thousand feet they were still in the shadow of cloud that dwarfed the sky with monstrous anvil-heads. The sun died within them and far below the sea became iron grey.

"They must be up around the seventeen thousand," Scott said beside Read. "Can you see your way over?"

Joe Read looked at his watch. He thought—We're for it anyway.

There was a half-conscious idea at the back of his mind that if he met this danger, it would be easier to face the other.

"Look, Clarry," he said: "I don't go much on taxiing around enemy anchorages in the dark. It's not my idea of a good time at all. So I'm going through the cloud. It shouldn't be too bad below that saddle there; and at seven thousand we'll clear the mountains by a couple of thou'. I've been through worse at night—but then you can't see them. At any rate, if I get into trouble, you work with me on the controls. But don't overpower me, you great brute."

The Catalina plunged into the cloud like a dragon-fly into the belly of a toppling wave.

Night lay like a kernel at the centre of the cloud. The Catalina groaned and staggered under the buffeting of invisible forces. The two pilots worked at the controls, their eyes never leaving the illuminated instruments. The miniature aircraft on the panel which portrayed the attitude of the flying-boat, stood on its port wing-tip. Both pilots applied full opposite aileron. A second passed and no answer came to the controls. Then as a wrestler will break from a clinch only to become locked in an alternative pose, the miniature aircraft flicked onto its starboard wing-tip and stayed there. At the same time the altimeter began to turn like the second-hand of a watch. They were in the up draughts.

Locked elbows braced the stick against the panel. The revolution of the altimeter slowed and the airspeed rose to two hundred knots. The two men sweated in the dark cockpit and slowly the rain and the darkness lessened. They broke cloud at fifteen thousand feet while their aircraft climbed in a diving attitude.

"So much for that."

Joe Read looked at Scott from mocking eyes that still showed rims of white.

"Thought we wouldn't come out of it, did you?" he said. "Mac! Is that our coffee you're standing in?"

"It is," said the engineer. "Sugared and all. And if we stay at this height, we'll have iced coffee for supper."

"Swab it up," said Read; "and make another lot. And crew: tidy up. We've got visitors."

He reduced power and commenced to circle down through the burnt-out cloud-columns to the northward. A blue twilight world lay below where the land was distinguishable from the sea only by its darker shadows. To port, like summer lightning, guns flickered.

"This is the right place, all right," Read said. He banked to starboard and heard the sudden sizzling on the stove. "Forget the coffee, Mac ... Can you raise the Mitchell, operator?"

As he spoke, a call came through with startling clearness like a voice in a seance.

"Are you receiving? Are you receiving? Michael calling Catfish: Go ahead. Over."

Read put aside his hand transmitter and slipped on his throat microphone.

"Michael from Catfish: Receiving you loud and clear. How are you receiving me? I am at three thousand feet, one mile east of Besar Island. Report your position. Over."

"Catfish from Michael: Receiving you loud and clear. I am two miles east of the town at one thousand feet. The dinghy is between me and the sunken ship. It is getting very difficult to see. I suggest that I drop two flame-floats north-south, and two east-west. The dinghy will be in the apex. Does that suit you? Over."

"Roger, Michael. Go ahead."

Thirty seconds later, Read saw two orange lights blossom on the surface of the sea. The shore batteries opened up on them.

"Looks pretty hot in there, Michael."

There was no reply until two more lights bloomed on the water, parallel with the coast.

"Right. There you are Catfish," Michael called. "Come right in now. You won't see them in another five minutes. I will be above you and direct you once you're down."

In the pale blue reflections of the instrument lighting, Read's face hardened, becoming tight with anger. Who was that bastard ordering him into his grave in the angle of those bobbing lights; not giving him a moment to consider? Apart from the guns, there was the sea; an iron swell to split the hull in the failing light; a stick of drift-wood from the wreck to rip them wide. Yet here was some ignorant fool with no knowledge of seamanship, making his decisions for him.

"You'd better stick above, Michael!" he said. "Floats, engineer."

The dim horizon tilted and slipped past their nose. There was the noise of running chains as the floats came down. Checking above the grey sea-hillocks, the two pilots looked straight ahead at the rapidly approaching illuminations of the guns.

The first Joss Brown in the Mitchell saw of the Catalina was a white line drawn on the grey sea; but by that time he had lost sight of the dinghy. He directed the Catalina to the apex of the triangle.

On the water Read was surprised by the strange normality of things. He might have been taxying to a buoy on the Middle Arm anchorage at Darwin. The sea lapped happily at the hull and looking across its grey expanse, he could see the converging reflections of the flares. As they neared the apex a column of water rose from under the nose and drenched the windscreen. They were under fire from the shore batteries. The explosion of the shells above the noise of the motors sounded like the popping of corks.

"Some party, eh, Skip?" said the navigator. His head and shoulders showed through the forward hatch. "There's the wreck straight ahead, but I'm damned if I can see the dinghy. Swing her starboard: there's something dark over there. Port: swing port. God! Nearly collected a burnt out launch, or something. I give up, Skip. I can't see a thing. And I don't go for this, much."

A moment later the Mitchell reported, "Can't see the dinghy, Catfish. How are you going down there. The guns have stopped firing."

Joe Read tasted the blood from his bitten lip. He said to himself: Easy, bloke; take it easy. Only one more turn round. He wanted to go home. His mind resisted the impulse of his body to jam the throttles through the gate and to take the flying-boat off. He did not like the stillness of the guns: It probably meant that launches were out after him. He had done all that was expected of him; to wait was suicide. And there was his crew to consider. One more turn round, he told his body. In the darkness he could not distinguish land from sea.

A brilliant ray of violet light lit up the sea to their port. A searchlight had been set up on the stern of the wreck. The light hesitated on the water and moved towards them.

Read felt a thump on his arm. Scott beside him was going through the actions of a hitch-hiker.

"Let's get out of here," he said.

"Dinghy to port!"

Read was swinging the Catalina to seaward on full starboard throttle when the cry came from his navigator. A hundred yards away, in the centre of the violet pathway, lay the yellow dinghy. Read sobbed as he taxied into the brilliance of the light. He turned his tail into the dinghy and at the same moment tracer flowed down the beam.

"Step on it," he said. "Have you got them? Have you got them?"

Down the long tunnel of the fuselage, he saw clambering men, now dark, now vivid, hauling dim shapes up through the sloping gun-blister.

A ten-second eternity ended. Word came, "Roger, Skip. Take her away!"

In a blinding violet world no bigger than a room, Read commenced his take-off. The reflected light from the windscreen hid the sea and only the instruments told him of his relative position. He fought the sea and wind at second hand, crying "Come up, you bitch; come up, you bastard!" The hull of the flying-boat struck the ridges of the swell and Read rode at the controls like a jockey. Joss Brown saw the Catalina leave its phosphorescent wake behind. It banked steeply into the darkness. The searchlight swept the deserted sea and went out.

"How are you going, Catfish?" he called. "Did you get them? Is Flight Lieutenant Ellis all right?"

A crackle came through the receiver; and then a voice from the darkness, flat with control: "Yes, we got them. Five are all right: shock and bruises. But Ellis is in a bad way. His left leg is shattered and he's badly burnt. That is all. And now"—with the voice rising—"shut up, will you? I'm going to have some coffee."

Joe Read found that he was shaking with anger,

sweating it. Why the devil hadn't he been told of this job earlier? He knew the reason: radio interference; but his fever annulled it. He crouched muttering and swearing among his cushions, gripping the wheel with his small hands until they showed white.

And when the engineer touched him on the shoulder, such an image of fear leapt in his mind—the shattering of the windscreen, a sick slackness in the controls—that he upset the coffee over his sleeve. He cursed the engineer for a clumsy fool.

But the coffee comforted him. They had climbed out of the sea-haze and the whole sky opened up around him, the familiar stars by which he checked his course. It was known territory. The motors beat their sweet three-second rhythm. And they were for home.

Beer and bed; beer and bed. The motors sang it. And the ditched crew were stowed safely in the bunks behind.

"Right-oh, Clarry," Read said. "You take over. And Mac: your coffee's improving. It was worth waiting for."

In the straight bunk aft, Ellis gripped his elephant mascot in bandaged hands and stared out into the night. He had never seen such stars.

And from the night a call came through: "Catfish from Michael! My petrol tank has been holed. I shall fly to Cartier Reef and crash-land there on the sea. Can you stand by? Over."

III

We'll All Jump in Together

The Mitchell climbed into the tall night and behind, gunfire spluttered out in haze. For the first time in many hours Joss Brown at the controls had time to think.

It was a moment he had dreaded. But coming back to himself, he was surprised by a feeling of relief. The fear that had turned at the back of his mind all day was no longer there.

It had been an unreasonable fear, a fear of landing at night on the tree-flanked strip back at base. Lately the eye of the flare-path had seemed so treacherously narrow.

And now a landing at base was out of the question. A bullet had pierced the auxiliary fuel tank and shortly he must crash-land the aircraft on the sea. It was an act of fate; something for which Brown did not feel responsible.

"Right-oh, crew," he said. "I want you all up the front. Right down the aisle, please. I'm levelling out; and we'll need to get our nose down to make Cartier Reef.—All except you, Johnnie. You stay by the wireless. And Les? I'm cutting back the airspeed to 150 knots."

The note of the engines slowed and broadened. The aircraft rode the top layer of an inversion. With a quick movement of his hand, Brown caught a small black fly against the window glass. He opened the window and let it out into the slipstream.

This action brought the night down around him. A

153

multitude of stars poured cold light into the cockpit and engraved the black tenuous folds of the haze below. Brown thought of the small fly lost in immensity. It led him to the edge of space. The earth turned beneath him and he was cut off from it; isolated among the stars.

He stared down into the haze. Somewhere down there, he must bring the aircraft back to earth. And tonight there would be no needle-eye of flares. Brown looked out into the darkness, thinking of a small black fly. Responsibility had returned.

A rough hand cuffed his shoulder.

"So you reckon you've won my beer ration, do you Joss?"

It was Bill Stanford, his tail gunner.

"I certainly do," Brown said.

There was still this small world within the shell of fuselage, and its relations with that other world.

"The ship was there: that was the bet. Still, I might give you half a glass."

"There's the generous Joss. But it was almost worth it. Do you know, as we went over, I met the ship's cook face to face: tall white cap and white apron; oh! a great spread! going over the rail like a hurdler. Funny the little things you see. Seemed a pity to shoot him."

"But you did?"

"There was a gun up forrard ... " Stanford said. "But look here, you great red idol! About that bet. Three thousand tons, we said. She didn't have it in her. That's my stance."

"Is it?" Brown said. "Well, you know what you can do? Jump in the lake."

"That's what I'm afraid of," Stanford said. "That's just it, boy. But you'll be with me! We'll all jump in together."

154

Stanford found this irresistably funny. He leaned his great weight between the seats, shaking them with his laughter.

"Eric doesn't drink," he said, clapping the second pilot between the shoulders. "You'll give me your beer, won't you Eric? I'll be right, you'll find."

He looked sideways at the young man's pale lonely face and offered him a cigarette.

"Go on," he said, "Do you good."

Eric Law shook his head. "I don't smoke thanks," he said.

Bill Stanford was about to laugh. Here we are, he thought, between life and death, and he still thinks it wrong to smoke. Probably promised his mother or something, remembering the photograph in their tent of a faded hawk-like beauty. If she could see her darling child now!

But Stanford did not laugh. He was looking at Law, wondering what he could say to the boy. There seemed to be not one thing in the whole world that he could say to him.

Alone, down the back Johnnie Roberts prepared for the ditching. Against the bulkhead he had stacked water-cans, rations, first-aid kits, distress signals, dinghies. And now he sat back with his feet on the water-cans, rolling a cigarette. He turned it in his fingers. It was perfect. He put it with the others in a water-tight tin and rolled tobacco in his dry palm.

Roberts believed in doing things well; and in being prepared. For instance, there was that clause in his will in case his wife married again.

He had drawn the will up himself, and in the comfort of legal phrases, had never really imagined his own death. But it was in the evidence and had to be provided for. He knew of so many cases ... And there were the children's interests to protect.

Now, confronted by death, he thought of his children. They crept giggling into his study while he worked. Would that be their memory of him? A precise man in a city suit—old to them, no doubt—nodding gravely while they showed him the dead robin; a man who turned on an impulse to jot down a thought, a phrase.

Suddenly he wanted to leave more than that, more than a dry image and a clause in a will. Leave what? Love, or its break-up, had brought in most of Robert's business.

He rolled another cigarette in the dim tail of the air-craft, thinking of his wife.

He found that the quality of his cigarettes had fallen off. This was no way to think. You made all prepara-tions; you took all precautions. And then you waited like this, as he had waited many times for the erratic verdict of the jury.

He looked at his watch and was busy for several minutes at the wireless.

"Wireless Operator to Navigator," he said: "Here's that radio fix: Darwin—Marauke."

He gave the bearings of both stations. In a moment Les St.John called back

"Nice work, Johnnie. That puts us within three miles of my dead-reckoning position."

"That so?" Roberts said dryly. "Then it must be wrong."

At the navigation table, St.John kept his head buried in his work. He had set himself a strict routine: a drift on a flame-float every ten minutes; three wireless-fixes and two star-fixes to the hour. His mind worked with the slow precision of a machine.

He brought a star into transit with the small glowing bubble in his sextant; he peered through the dark bombing panel at the lonely tongue of the flare flickering on the sea far below; and he tried to regard them as purely navigational aids. But at times the night came in; and then he muttered to the black mists, "Thy will be done." He groped his way back to his seat, comforted.

Suddenly he realized that there was nothing more for him to do. He crawled through to the windy nose and gazed steadily out into the darkness. He was looking for the reef.

"We should be there in four minutes now, Joss. Think we should start losing height? The haze seems to be thinning a little."

"All right," Brown said. "I'll take her down to two thousand feet. And crew: Go back to your normal positions and keep a good look out."

The aircraft nosed down towards the sea where the stars were reflected in the clear patches between the haze. The panel clock ticked off three minutes.

"What's that to starboard?"

"What do you think, Les?"

Towards the indistinct horizon, a black shape lay on the dark sea.

"May be it, Joss. Better have a look. I thought it would show white at night though."

Brown turned starboard, checked his petrol. He thought—If this isn't it, we're done for. Was he right to turn? Even death, it seemed, did not come without an agony of doubt.

After five minutes flying, they were in the shadow of a heavy cloud.

"Cloud shadows," Brown said. "Right, Les take us back onto track. Johnnie, get us a radio fix and go onto distress ditching procedure. The rest of you take up your ditching positions. We've about another ten minutes in the air."

He turned the aircraft through one hundred and eighty degrees and flew back onto track. The reflections of the stars were like the lights of a great city. The lights dimmed and they were back in the haze.

"We'll run down track for three minutes," Brown said; "Step aside for two and then run north for five. All right, Les?"

"All right," St.John said. "We're within five or six miles of the reef anyway. Those bloody cloud shadows."

"Don't worry, Les," Brown said. "Not your fault. It's the haze. The sea looked calm enough in that clear patch. She'll be right, you'll find."

Brown's mind had suddenly cleared. He was surprised by his own detachment. It was almost as if this was not happening to him at all. He was able to stand aside, without doubts or fears. For his way was clear.

They ran directly over the reef at their second turning point. The reef showed for a moment as a slight whitening of the sea and then was lost.

"Right-oh, Les," Brown said: "Ditching position. We've no time to drop flame-floats. Wind is what? South-east? Right. I'll swing her around and land towards the reef. All right, blokes, going down now. Keep calling the altitude, Eric."

"Fifteen hundred feet."

This was the worst that could happen.

"Thirteen hundred."

And he had worried about a flare path.

"Eleven."

Brown flashed the headlights for a moment. They were reflected back by the haze. The darkness was preferable.

"Five hundred feet."

He caught a glimpse of stars on the water. They gave a false impression of infinite depth. With his eyes on the instruments, he eased the tail down, the speed back, holding the aircraft up on the throttles. And he prepared for his final duty—to drag the stick into his belly as they touched.

"Zero."

With great force the aircraft struck the invisible sea. The second impact was heavier. The aircraft skidded for some distance and broke in half before diving below the surface.

The rising tide lapped about Joss Brown's feet and woke him from a cramped sleep. He sat up, pulled the parachute silk about him and blinked with tired eyes at the grey light moving slowly across the sea on the tide. Standing, he looked down at the four huddled figures of his crew. They were on higher sand so he did not wake them. But as he turned towards the dinghy, Les St.John joined him.

"How are you feeling, Les?' he asked. "It will be light soon. I'm having another search. Give me a hand with the dinghy."

They paddled the rubber raft out over the shallow ripples on the reef. Through the dull water dim clusters of coral flowered, and as the water deepened, they strained their eyes for any sign of white metal.

"This would be about the place," St.John said. "I

remember after thrashing the sea and getting nowhere, I put down my foot and was able to stand."

"The tide's risen since then," Brown said. "And it wasn't so shallow. I was caught up under the kite, gulping water and petrol, and didn't know which way was up. Just as well the dinghy floated, I'd say."

"Oh, you could stand," St.John said.

They smiled wearily at one another, thinking of the night before when they had floundered and cursed in the dark water until finally five of them had clambered into the dinghy. There they had waited, helloing across the star-pricked stillness for Stanford and Roberts until the moon rose.

By moonlight they searched for several hours, picking up water-cans and parachute packs but no sign of the missing men. Worn out, they paddled to the thin crescent of sand within the reef and, huddled together, slept.

Now they searched again but without hope. Their two friends had flown with them for nearly a year and this was the end of it. The chill half light brought bitterness and pain. They paddled the dinghy in silence, each wondering if the other blamed him.

—Am I to blame? Brown wondered. Yes. I should have checked the petrol earlier. And even then, had we left Ellis, we could have got home. I should have thought of my own crew first. Yet at the back of his mind, there was a new firmness.

They found the forward section of the aircraft in ten feet of water. Brown stripped off and dived into the clean sea. He came up with his lungs aching but his head clear. He dived again and searched among the wreckage in the green twilight.

Back in the dinghy, he saw for the first time the

colours climbing the sky. The high clouds glowed with the morning sun and the sea was bright with light. Unwillingly, Brown felt a surge of joy and strength in his tired body.

"There's only half the kite there," he said. "You have a go, Les."

St.John stripped and plunged. A multitude of bubbles broke the surface and St.John himself came up, spitting water. He dived again and Brown laughed helplessly in the dinghy while the bubbles rose. They paddled to deeper water, looking for the tail unit.

In the cascading light the coral beds revealed their delicate changing colours. Small multi-toned fish swam from green water above white sand to the deep opaque blue beyond.

"Look at this one, Les," Brown said. "Have you ever seen such colours? Look at those flecks of red light; and there, bright gold!"

"I wouldn't mind a bit of that coral to take home," St.John said.

"I'll get you some."

Brown dived again, this time in search of treasure. The cool sea closed around him and he opened his eyes to marvel at its submarine splendours. Somewhere, where the blue deepened, his two friends lay drowned. That he accepted now. Life had moved on.

They spent the next half-hour searching for colours and diving. Almost ashamed of their happiness at being alive, they paddled towards the sand. The sun burnished the sea and a small object caught the light among the ripples at the water's edge. The dinghy grounded beside a stout tobacco tin. Brown opened it and found a dozen dry, perfectly rolled cigarettes and some water-proof matches. They looked at one another in wonder.

"Yours, Les?"

"No. Yours, Joss?"

"No. But what are we waiting for?"

As the blue smoke curled on their breath they knew perfect happiness. Johnnie Roberts had left more than a clause in a will.

Further down the beach the other three were waving wildly and pointing to the east. Brown and St.John turned to hear the low distant rhythm of aircraft engines. A Catalina came out of the sun. Arm in arm they walked up the beach to join their waving crew.

"How will bacon and eggs go?" said St.John.

"All right," said Brown. "And we'll share Bill Stanford's beer."

Zero at Rabaul

We met the sun half-way that morning, on the leg from Seven Mile to Hood Point, before we turned north-east to cross the Owen Stanleys. We were climbing to gain height for the crossing, our aircraft very heavy and sloppy with its extra petrol load and, as we gained the height of the parallel line of near blue mountains, the sun shot above the darker outline of the distant range. It was day; and I looked at it with mistrust.

I was not at all happy about the job we were on and I knew my second pilot felt the same way. Harry had been unusually quiet that morning as we ate our warm beans and drank hot tea from scalding pannikins; and that was unlike Harry. I didn't like Harry to be quiet.

We were to do a daylight recco of Kavieng and Rabaul. We were to return if there was no cloud cover. That was all very well on paper, written out in Ops Room in Gordon's neat hand: return if no cloud cover. But in the first place, when you are as inexperienced as I was then, you do not like returning empty-handed to the Cat. boys waiting for your information before taking off.

Then again, in spite of a bad weather report—fine and cloudless, visibility twenty miles—supposing there were cloud cover over the target. I could only expect it to be scattered at that time of the day, and over the land. That left a clear sea crossing from New Ireland to

Rabaul with both Jap fighter nests well stirred up. I had sampled the Kavieng fighters several nights before when Dick dived his Cat. into cloud with three of them spitting fire on his tail; a cloud which, my navigation told me, contained a four-thousand-foot peak. I waited for the bump or the shells to burst, and when neither came, I agreed with Dick that I would take the chance of the bump in preference any time.

It was the sea crossing now that had me worried, for I reasoned this way: If we went to Kavieng first and made our get-away through cloud down New Ireland, we would then have to cross in the open to Rabaul, whose fighters no doubt would be expecting us. And it was unpleasant to be expected in the open in those days. So my plan was this: To visit Rabaul first and then turn due west for fifty miles as if returning home. This would be over the land and I could expect some cloud support. Fifty miles west I intended to turn north-east, run over Kavieng, lose height through cloud to tree-top height and make my get-away due west low over the water. When out of danger I intended to set course for Salamaua.

That was my plan; I had thought it out during an air raid the night before while Jap bombers circled unmolested above the moonlit cirrus. And I went over it again now as we climbed towards the range.

The sun seemed to climb faster than we did. Its light slanted down into the undulating lowlands beneath us so that the ridges separated themselves sharply from the darkness of the valleys and stood defined like the ribs of some gigantic fossil. Wisps of low cloud added to this effect. It was as if some cotton wool tufts had remained stuck to the bones after their unpacking. Jungle covered the ribs and knotted backbone like moss. This country had been dead a long time.

We crossed the main range at ten thousand feet. Clouds were already coming up to meet us, clambering from the peaks like apes into the higher air. This was a good sign but meant that they would be above fifteen thousand for our return. Over Buna the clouds broke, leaving only blueness before us; blue sea and blue air. A coral reef scarred the sea under our starboard wing, looking for the moment like the wake of a ship. In the distance a Gothic cumulus like a crazy scarecrow sat on air. We checked our guns, lined up the I.C., Harry gave the camera a final check. We felt better now that we were on the way.

I remembered Bob. He had taken off on a job somewhat like this about a week before. I drove up from the town over the dusty road with his operation order. He read through it but he seemed all the time to be thinking of something else. He waved his hand and took off. I have always liked watching a Hudson take off. Until its wheels are up it seems to be pulled off the ground by sheer brute force. You can hear the horses straining. Then the wheels tuck themselves up in three slow jerks and the aircraft begins to fly. A Hudson looks very good with its wheels up as it skims the trees at the beginning of its climb. But I watched that day with a different emotion. Bob would not come back. I was convinced of it. And standing there on the tender roof watching the dust settle and Bob turning on to course, I think I felt more emotion than he did. I know I felt more disturbed then than when I was ordered out on this job. We were talking over a bottle of warm beer of what we would do on leave in Sydney when Pedro came up and in his slow way told me I was to go out next morning. I felt fear immediately. But you do not write yourself off in your own mind with the finality with which I wrote off Bob from the top of the truck that day. Your mind always brings you home, damaged perhaps, but alive, from its most daring fantasies. As well as this, you have other things that must be thought over. When I dismissed Bob, I had time to pause, to allow the luxury of sadness to shape itself. Confronted with the same risk myself, there was my plan to think out, my aircraft to be teed up, so that my immediate fear was pushed to the back of my mind and became a vague apprehension which sharpened all actions. This apprehension sits buried in the mind, ready to flare into sudden fear when an enemy convoy is sighted or fighters appear. It acts as a spur and a warning to caution. It is like the sign at a railway crossing: "Danger. Beware of trains."

I called up Harry on the I.C.

"Do you see anything there, dead ahead?"

"Where? Fighters?"

"Cloud."

"Whacko."

Cloud lay over the highlands of New Britain, massed cloud, yellow with distance. Like robbers who see an open church door, we headed for it.

We made landfall at Gasmata. The runways were deserted, pockmarked with bomb craters. I remembered that the Wirraway boys had landed there on their way to Rabaul. Two of them, slowed up by the long grass, had hit their tail wheels in the water taking off. The grass had been mown since then and the Wirraway boys had been shot down in seven minutes over Rabaul.

It was not far from Gasmata to the highlands over which the cloud crawled. I had marked the same route on the maps of the Wirraway pilots and they had been warned that they were to take the coastal route if the day were cloudy. Cloud had taken on a different meaning since then. It was no longer to be avoided. Its down draughts, its ice, and its magnetic storms were forgotten when fighters were about. We wrapped its greyness around us and felt secure. The wing-tips became our farthest horizon.

Harry came up with chocolate. We munched and watched the water stream from our wings. It trickled into my boots. I felt happy.

"How long to go?"

"Should be there in thirty-six minutes," Harry said.

"Thirty-six?"

"And a half," said Harry. And he joined his thumb and forefinger as if throwing a dart.

Ten minutes before E.T.A. I checked the fuel. The auxiliary tank was almost empty, leaving the main tanks full. I changed to left front and once more checked all instruments. The aircraft with its reduced load handled better now. The clouds were still thick but they broke occasionally, revealing patches of rain-soaked jungle ten thousand feet below. The next break revealed the coast south of Wotom Island. We were almost there. For a moment I mistook a small island for an aircraft carrier and we circled. Then we swung back onto course for Rabaul.

As we broke cover the harbour lay several miles ahead and below us. The cloud formed a crescent to the south and to the east, leaving the harbour clear except for scattered high, fair-weather cumulus. In the distance I could see the blue outline of New Ireland.

We made our camera run directly over Rabaul township, turned at the Beehives and swung around

167

over Lakunai. There were about thirty ships in the harbour. Three destroyers lay in a triangle where I had seen them two days previously. There were a further three destroyers in harbour and the merchant-men were dispersed at anchor in approximately two scattered lines. Further construction work had been done on the building area at the lower drome. There were small grey and brown aircraft lined along both sides of the runways and the flying boats lay with their noses into wind outside the mouth of the river. The only movement I could see was that of a crazy little tug which circled and twisted in the harbour mouth. Not an A/A burst was fired.

I counted the number of ships, noting their disposition and types on a small map I had of the harbour. I counted the number of flying boats. But all the time another part of my mind was noting other things. It noted the sunlight on the harbour, the dots of the coconut trees, the slow smoke rising from the brown-fissured mouth of Matupi. That part of my mind would not be convinced that there was a war on this soft spring morning. As far as it was concerned I was not five hundred miles from home over enemy territory. And I found myself ready to laugh at the crazy panic of that little tug.

Then I saw the Zero. It was taking off from Lakunai, a small silver T pulling up over the tops of the coconut palms. I thought quickly. I had not quite finished the recco and I had at the most four minutes before the Zero gained our height. I warned the crew and put the aircraft into a steep turn over the harbour making my final notes.

Three minutes had elapsed since the Zero took off and I was just straightening from the turn, headed for cloud, when I felt a sudden hammer blow on my left wrist and pins and needles in my hand. At the same moment the instrument panel began to fall to pieces. I looked at my wrist in surprise. Where my watch had been there was a round blue hole. The palm of my hand was ripped open and the end of my little finger was missing. The bullet had evidently come from behind, penetrated my wrist, passed through the control wheel—there was an inch gap in its circumference—and taken off my little finger before lodging in the airspeed indicator.

And I was surprised; completely surprised. I am convinced that a man, until he sees bullets flying around him, does not basically realize that war is serious, that the enemy is out to kill him. Height detaches the bomber pilot from actual violence. He runs over a ship; four small darts slide from the belly of his aircraft and disappear below. Looking down he sees a plume of smoke start from the stricken ship and he congratulates himself on his good bombing. He knows little of the panic and destruction where his small darts have struck. He has lived a normal peaceful life and he is immune from this until his instrument panel begins to fall apart and he sees his hand flapping suddenly like a dying fish.

I looked at the waving of my hand with surprise and a certain nausea. Then I glanced around into the aircraft cabin. It was filled with smoke. This I thought is the end. And again I was filled with a strange surprise; surprise that I, having done and thought the things that make up my particular existence, should end my life here in a burning aircraft ten thousand feet above a town I had lived in not a month back. For I felt no doubt that this was the end. It was a visible fact. It took this to convince the subtleties of my imagination that I was as vulnerable as Bob.

During the second that this thought filled my mind, my hand had jammed the throttles through the gate, loosened the catch of the emergency exit and the aircraft was diving for cloud while my feet jumped alternately on left and right rudder. I heard the turret guns open up again and in my mind I saw the silver fighter diving in for its second attack. Ken Erwin had given me an image of a Zero attacking. He was attacked head on. Vapour flags streamed from either wing-tip and smoke from the forward guns. I saw this image now. Glass fell once more from the instrument panel and then grey cloud immersed us; we were soaked in cloud.

No flames belched from the cabin so with the vision of that silver fighter still on our tail, I kept the aircraft in its dive, turning steeply one way, straightening up and turning the other. I thought of mountains, but they did not worry me. We had been in cloud at least a minute before I realized that I was flying without instruments. I cleaned the compass of a film of silver dust and found we were once more headed for Rabaul. I cleaned the artificial horizon and, levelling out, turned due west following my original plan. The airspeed indicator and both altimeters were shot away. Several other instruments were missing, but the petrol, air temperature and one cylinder head temperature gauge were undamaged as were the rev and boost counters. I noted that the smoke was not increasing but still hung in the air like silver dust. Then I saw Harry.

Harry had been busy with the camera when he noticed a large portion of the tail unit disappear. At the same time he felt a concussion in his body. Looking at the camera he thanked God that it had not been hit. He struggled into his parachute harness and not until he had walked up to the W/T cabin, where he suddenly sat down, did he realize how badly he was wounded. His right index finger was shot away and his second finger hung down his palm from a thin cord. His left arm was paralysed from a bullet lodged in his biceps, and blood flowed from a large hole in the calf of one leg. He sat there unable to move while smoke curled around him. Looking at his damaged hand he wondered how the devil he had managed to clip on his parachute harness.

It was there that Jock found him. Jock was in the bomb aimer's position taking notes when bullets began to whistle above his head and he saw them spraying out past the nose. We discovered later that there were two hundred and sixty odd holes in the aircraft from the two attacks. Jock climbed the companionway and, seeing Harry, he turned and was sick down the companionway. When I saw Harry I felt no emotion whatsoever. I was hit; I thought the aircraft was on fire; in half-a-minute it had been turned from an orderly unit into a butcher's shop. I thought and felt certain things for a few overwhelming seconds. And then my emotions ceased to function. Like so many good coal miners, they went on strike. I looked at Harry and told myself that it was only to be expected. Jock, however, knowing little of what had happened, was taken by surprise. His system rebelled against the evidence of his eyes and he was sick.

Immediately afterwards he got to work. He cleaned up the sea-marker that had been hit and was filling the aircraft with aluminium dust. He put out some smouldering ammunition. He came forward to fix me up. A tourniquet made from wireless leads proved too painful for my arm so he wrapped it up in a shirt and left it at that. He told me that our rear gunner had got it on both legs and he went back to fix him up.

I am not sure whether the rear gunner lost sight of the Zero during my steep turn or whether he was following the inexperienced instructions I had given him earlier that he was to pick up as much information as possible while we were over the target. Nor am I sure whether the Zero that attacked us was the one I saw taking off or whether another had dived from high cloud cover while we were watching the former. At all events the attacker was already pressing home his attack when our gunner saw him. He warned me then but the I.C. had already been hit. He got in a good burst as the Zero pulled away, showing his belly, and although wounded, fought it out during the next attack. He estimated that the Zero must have received fairly extensive damage. He did not leave the turret until we were well out of danger in the cloud. A concentrated burst of explosive cannon had ripped a large hole in the turret just between his open knees.

We came into the clear about thirty miles west of Rabaul. I judged that we were about two thousand feet above the jungle. There were storm clouds to the south-east so I turned into them for home. It was then that Harry surprised me. Sitting in his blood he asked if we were going on the Kavieng. Going on to Kavieng! This thought had not even entered my head. I was going home. Directly I saw my hand flapping, out of control, to get home or as near home as possible, had become instinctive. And now Harry asked me if we were going on. Then I understood him. Harry had not expected to return from this job. And I realized that, at the back of my mind, I hadn't either. I grinned at Harry and he grinned back and we seemed to say to one another: "Well, we've been shot up but we're going home. Things weren't so bad after all."

But could we make it? In the clear I had taken stock of the damage. The engines were going well but there were several bullet holes through the cowlings. And all the tanks were leaking. I was shocked to find that one tank was using more fuel than the one I was running on. Next, could I make it myself? I felt the blood from my arm dribbling from its shirt wrapping into my boots as the rain had, happily, an hour previously. Fear kept me from looking at my wound again. I wanted to keep it shut away from myself.

I tried to reason with my instinct to head for Moresby. Salamaua was closer. And there was no fifteen thousand feet crossing. But there was no doctor as far as I knew at Salamaua, only a small detachment of New Guinea Riflemen; communication between Salamaua and Moresby had been out of order that morning before we left; it was unlikely that an aircraft would be able to get over there that day. I told myself this but I knew that I would head for Moresby, anyway. If the fuel was low before the range crossing, I would divert to Salamaua.

So our return became a race for time against the leaking fuel. I could no longer nurse the motors. Here was another excuse. With the throttles open to the gate, I eased up the nose and began to climb in the general direction of Port Moresby. By this time we had already gained some height and the boost was little more than twenty-eight inches.

I tried out George. Although the directional gyro was damaged, the bank and climb held. I looked around the cockpit. Everything was covered with a thin layer of silver, instruments, controls, and even Jock's face as he lit a cigarette and put it in my mouth. My small map of Rabaul had been shot out of my hand, and this with the maps of the whole area was covered in blood and silver dust.

I drew on the cigarette and began to cipher a message to base. Half-way through Harry called to me that the engines were losing power. The manifold pressures were falling rapidly. So we were for it after all. It would have been better to finish at Rabaul than crash-land here through cloud in the central New Britain jungle. But it might be ice. Rime was frosting the windscreen and wings. I put in the carburettor heats. The roar of the engines opened out again; the manifold pressures built up. Time once more moved forward. Jock was going over the wireless. He came forward and told me it had been damaged. I put aside the recco report and sat back looking into the greyness. As we gained height things seemed to matter less and less. My arm lost all feeling and lay numb and still on my knee. And as the ache receded, so the meaning began to slip away from this race against fuel.

We came out of cloud high over the jungle to the northward of Gasmata. The sea was bright with sun and the outline of the coast disappeared westward in blue haze. I found myself saying: "Don't let there be any fighters." It would be necessary then to swing the aircraft around, dive for the yellow cloud over the highlands, creep west through cloud with the fuel gauges falling. Here, with the aircraft climbing, I could sit back in the sun where nothing very much seemed to matter. I began to think of home.

I had been thinking of home only the night before and now, no doubt, I would be sent home. My wife and I would take a flat at King's Cross, a flat high up overlooking the harbour. We would stay in bed late and when we got up we would wander around the shops in the sun buying fruit and salads and cold meats. We would take them back to the flat and there would be cold beer on the ice and the day would be both cool and warm so that we needn't wear a great deal. And the curtains would blow in occasionally in the wind from the harbour.

I pulled myself together with a start and slapped myself several times hard on the side of the face. I checked the gauges and the course. I could see the cloud now over the Owen Stanleys and I knew I had been wise to keep her climbing. It was towering above the range in great sunlit ramparts. There were eighty gallons in the right rear tank as we crossed the coast on course north of Buna. Salamaua lay to the right in a sun haze.

Climbing still, we had to divert slightly to the south to avoid the tops of the cumulus. I judged that we were at about eighteen thousand feet; the temperature gauge read below zero, but I was taking no chances now of hitting the hills. Beyond the cumulus tops lay a wide cloud layer whose brilliant whiteness hurt the eyes. There were occasional breaks.

Harry said: "We must be about there." He had not moved from his position on the floor and his hand looked grotesque.

I throttled back and nosed the aircraft down through a wispy cloud break. And there below, ringed in storm, lay Port Moresby. I checked the gauges before diving. There were forty gallons; petrol to spare.

Diving, I hoped the tail unit would hold. We spiralled, passing through scattered rain and wispy cloud. And all the time below lay Moresby, the hillsides baked brown and grey by sun; its inlets and islands defined as on a map; the sea glassy, coloured by strips of green shallows; but ruffled and wind-lined to the north-west by a sudden squall. We got into the rain from the squall and I pulled out fifty feet from the water over the light in the harbour mouth. In the clear we headed for Seven Mile. I checked the tanks and we had five gallons of fuel left in one tank. All the others read empty. The change of pressure in the dive must have opened the holes in the tank and let the petrol out. I had two alternatives: To land the aircraft on the water in the harbour or to try to make Seven Mile. We headed for Seven Mile. If we didn't make it, it still did not matter a great deal. On the water there was every chance of Harry and our gunner drowning, if not all of us.

We sneaked over the coastal hills and there in the valley between its rough skirting ranges was Seven Mile. Jock was beside me. I put down the under-carriage and it clicked home. We checked the wheels visually. They looked all right. The trim I found had been shot away. We turned in for the approach. I had not had time or fuel to check the flaps higher up so I decided to put them down and if the aircraft swung, to bring them straight up again.

"Right, flaps," I called to Jock.

Jock pressed down the flap lever and at the same moment my port engine coughed and spluttered. The aircraft swung heavily to port. The starboard engine coughed.

It then became necessary to do a number of things. It really did not matter. We would land on our guts in the scrub-covered gully but these things had to be done first.

"Up with flaps."

I shoved the nose forward keeping the speed at what I judged to be ninety knots. I took the stick in my left hand and power seemed to come back to it. With my right, I changed to another tank, for there might be a few gallons left, and pumped hard on the wobble pump. The engines coughed, picked up. Still priming, we cleared a pile of petrol drums and the wheels touched on the runway. As the aircraft ran down the gravelled strip, she seemed to limp and there was a thudding sound of rubber.

"The starboard tyre's gone."

"All right." It did not matter any more. I got my left arm over the stick, holding it back and the left aileron down. With my right hand I pulled on the brake, counteracting swing with full left rudder. The tail kicked, came down and the aircraft slowed up. Slowly it turned and stopped at right angles to the runway.

"Right, cut."

The engines cut and there was stillness.

Now out, out of this aircraft, get your feet on ground. I stumbled through the silver-coated cabin, out of the door into the sunlight.

I began walking rapidly towards the huts which stood amongst slender gum trees on the other side of the runway. A tender swung through dust from the hut road making for the aircraft. I waved it on. My feet had taken control of me and it was as if they were off to catch a train. They would not stop. I did not realize what a spectacle I must have looked, carrying my hand still wrapped in a shirt, my face and hands and knees coloured silver as if badly burnt. Pedro leapt from the side of the tender. A car drew up and he pushed me in. My tongue immediately took over from my legs. I was still talking rapidly when we pulled up outside the main hut.

There I made my report to Col. It was a relief to be able to talk without interruption. My tongue ran forward, detailing the ships in the harbour, the construction work on the lower drome while Col scribbled notes on a pad, trying to keep up. Men stood around, their fingers still marking the places in their magazines where they had been reading. Pedro offered me brandy but I refused. That, I told myself, would be the end. If only I can keep on talking. If I keep talking I won't break down.

An hour later, in hospital, I was happier than I have ever been. I was washed and clean, ready for the operation. My arm was not painful and I felt slightly drunk at still being alive. And I was going home. The army nurses seemed unbelievably beautiful.

Foxes Don't Wait

When John Clement drew a block under the mountains and went to settle there, the stillness was strange to him. He bought a prefab. hut from the army for twenty pounds and set it up on a sheep-camp among lazy gum-trees. The only reason he worked so hard at it was to break the monotony. Whenever he paused, leaned on the ridgepole, and looked out across the pepper and salt paddocks, his mind stopped work too. The sunlight fell down from the bleached sky like a backdrop; the trees stood still; the only movement was the thin shimmer of heat, on a humped horizon. He had an impulse to climb down and shake the trees with his hands. The countryside was like a dream and he was the sleep-walker. He wondered how long he could stand this clambering about on a still life.

When the hut was finished, he furnished it like the flight office up north: a couple of stretchers, aircraft photographs, the shattered blade of an enemy fighter; and wired for his wife. They had married late in the war and had been separated so often that he hardly knew her. After a week in the hut, she decided that she did not know him at all.

It was the fox that woke him up, leaping through his numbness like a lion through a paper hoop.

He was riding at noon through a litter of stumps and fallen timber when his horse suddenly shied and stood alert and trembling under his heel. John Clement swore, sat still. Intent in the fanged shade ahead, a fox crouched, lithe and red. It was being attacked by magpies.

The magpies stalled high in the clear air in a flurry of feathers; winged over, and came in sleekly, steeply, down the shafts of light. The brush of the fox pulsed, tipped with white, and it snap-snapped, over its shoulder at the passing birds. Its quiet body was curled and poised like a flexed spring.

Clement relaxed in the saddle and a clear light leapt in his eyes. He was watching the tactics of the birds. They came in together, one out of the sun, the other low and swiftly from between the trees. And the fox sprang softly in a gyre with sneered back lips. It turned and trotted low through the blonding grass, trailing its brush. And in a gust of wind, the whole hillside seemed to move like the fur on the animal.

Clement galloped home through the living grass to get his rifle.

In the hut he found his wife swaying through brightly lit halls in a new silk dress. Auburn light flickered in her brushed hair and there were flecks of gold in brown eyes.

"How do I look?" she said, swaying.

"Just seen a fox," Clement said. "Where's my rifle? God damn it, Jo: what have you done with it this time?"

"Sit down, just for a minute, and admire me. And then I'll tell you."

"Look, Jo, foxes don't wait indefinitely,"

But he sat down.

"Do you like it?" Jo was standing with her legs apart, looking down at herself. She smoothed her thighs. Then lifting straight eyes she said, "What's happened to you, anyway? You look like you used to look."

"Try the other," Clement said.

And when the skirt was over her head so that she was tied up in silk, Clement picked her up laughing and laid her down struggling among the boxes and tissue-paper on the bed. It was the first time they had been really happy since the war.

Later Clement said, "You know that fox, Jo? I don't think I'll shoot it after all. There's something about that fox I rather like. It's alive."

And he smoothed her rusted hair with forgotten tenderness.

"You're as cunning as a fox yourself," Jo said. "Try the other one!" Clement saw the fox quite often through the summer and autumn of that year. On the stone hill, going through the sheep for fly, he would look up, and there on a ledge where brittlejacks grew gold and naked towards the light, would be the fox. Its incurious stare, surprised there in sunlight, and surprising, pleased him. The fox lived its own life and he lived his. And the gold trees grew from stone.

Clement was no longer mocked by the stillness, by an image of fruitless eternity, through the long quiet days. There was a sense of growth, of strife; and life was hard and joyous.

"You know..." he said one night, lying on his back and listening to the magpies singing to the full moon. All around the hut he could hear his sheep cropping the grass with a soothing sound like the slapping of small waves. The fog rolled around the valley like a tide.

"I know what?" Jo said.

"Listen to the magpies, Jo."

"Do I know what?" Jo sat up in bed and began tickling him. "I won't stop until you tell me."

"Well I'll tell you...to stop."

And they fought, "Oh no you don't," laughing, until Clement pinned her strong hands and kissed her.

"There," he said. "That's it. No, not quite. Almost: Better try again."

"What do you mean: not quite: almost? No John, not until you tell me."

"Jo, you look sweet by moonlight. You can't see your freckles. Let me see your face. One there, there..."

"No John, you must tell me."

"But I love your freckles, Jo."

He was surprised by his own sincerity. Beauty is a complete thing. Often for its blemishes he felt the greater tenderness.

"No, John."

Clement tossed onto his back and read DI, DI, by moonlight on the roof sections of the hut.

"You wouldn't understand," he said. "It's just this; that sometimes when we make love, I feel very close to the animals; and that this is right. The fox in its red cave under the hill is probably doing the same thing."

"And to the trees?" Jo said.

"Yes. And to the trees."

"And the flowers?"

"All right," Clement said.

"No, but really John: we're not foxes. We can't go on living this way indefinitely; not in this hut."

"You know the set-up about materials," Clement said. "They're all on order. It's no use panicking."

"But John, you don't try. You ride around all day thinking of your sheep—and of that damned fox. I've watched you. But what about me? Sometimes the

182

thought of that fox gets on my nerves."

"They're all on order," Clement said.

"Winter's coming, John. And what if we should have a baby?"

"We're not having a baby," Clement said. "So why talk about it?"

He turned over and for a long while felt his wife's body lying frozen at his side. About midnight the sheep scattered from around the hut with a sound like leaves in a gale. He heard his sheepdog rattle a ghost-chain, startling the night with its barking; and nearby, from among the pallid gum-trees, the yap of a fox.

The next morning it was as though the moonlight had frozen. The summer grass swept the hill like spindrift, dissolving in the light; the chips around the woodheap were furred; in shadow, the valley lay dead under the frost.

Jo Clement was sick in the bathroom lean-to in a bucket of ice. But she said nothing to her husband. He drove off to town to see about materials.

And winter came down.

"You do nothing; nothing," Jo said.

The wind swept out of a desolate centre and bellowed like a lost calf under the piles of the hut.

"Nothing; nothing."

They were sitting crouched around the squat stove for warmth. Clement looked at his wife's flat hair and was reminded of dead grass. Her eyes had become still and secretive. He stood up.

"I can't do more," he said. "The shed will be finished next month. I'll line it and it'll be better than here. I can't do more until the builders come. And it's no use trying to lay iron in this wind."

"Shed!" Jo said. "A pig wouldn't live in it. And what

were you doing all summer? Moping about thinking of foxes."

Malice struck a match in her eyes.

"Christ! I've had enough," Clement said.

He stalked out into the wind.

There, perched, battering at the shed's skeleton, he looked out across the valley at his stone hill. A scrap of snow had fallen on its weather side. He rode out and found his first winter lamb. The ewe stood with her tail into the wind and the lamb butted between the sheep's front legs. Clement was tempted to catch the ewe and put the lamb on her dugs. He rode the lambing paddocks and turned home.

The birth of their first lamb brought them closer together; and that evening, hunched over the stove, Jo watched him curiously.

"I think I know what you meant that night," she said. "I'm sorry I nagged."

"Which night was that?"

Clement was busy in the globe of light about the oil lamp, working out an estimate of the coming lambing.

"With any luck", he said, "We'll have eight hundred lambs this year. Then there'll be no trouble about getting a house built." He looked over at his wife.

She was sitting, her knees slightly spread, by the open grate, gazing through wide pupils into the warm heart of the coals.

"That's what I make it: eight hundred lambs."

The next morning he found twelve dead lambs curled in the frost.

There were frosts for seven days, hard frosts, under high still cloud, that set till mid-day in the hollows and scarred the ground. As they melted the grass seemed to melt away with them. On the seventh day, Clement's ewes in the hill paddock began to go down.

The crows found them first.

When he rode out over the hill on his morning round, there were more crows in the paddock than sheep. He went from one cluster of shining birds to the other, the birds hopping, spry, lifting out the wool with forcep-beaks and striking for the live eye and kidney. At his approach, they scattered like flung soot onto the dead limbs of the trees. Their cries were harsh, and colder than the frosts. And their eyes were blue.

Clement rode home for his skinning knife.

He skinned four cast ewes, dressed the eye sockets of two others, and carried three lambs home. He found them on the hillside butting for milk at the trunks of trees while crows waited on the limbs.

Jo treated them as if they were her own children.

"Look at him, John", she said. "Look at his tail. Doesn't it go?"

She was kneeling by the stove and the lamb was feeding from her fingers in a basin of warm milk, his foal-legs braced and his tail tying itself in bows. Clement looked down at his wife. Behind the tenderness in her eyes was a glint of something else, of fierce and stubborn protectiveness.

Twice that night she woke him up.

"Are they warm John? Have a look. Is the bag over them?"

"For God's sake, Jo", Clement said. "I've got to be up before dawn tomorrow."

Riding over the hill at the hungry hour, the trees stealthy, the light swelling up behind, and hearing the crack and break of ice under hooves, Clement found three cast ewes before the crows. A fourth had lost an eye and when he delivered her lamb, he found that its tongue had been pecked out. He swung it against a log, wondering how much his horse understood of it.

He skinned the ewe, punching off the luminous skin with his fist, and looked down at the stripped frame, its shell of ribs and oyster coil of guts.

All morning he followed the crows and at lunchtime rode home with one lamb kicking on the pommel.

When he reached the hut, he thought that his wife had gone crazy. Her face had fallen to pieces and she was in hysterics. Her red hair, damp from weeping, hung in knots about her cheeks.

"Take it away," she cried. "Don't bring it here. Don't dare!"

"But Jo..."

"Don't dare."

He let the lamb go and it nuzzled around the hind legs of his horse. In the hut he found the three lambs as if sleeping in their warm box by the stove. He touched a shining doll's-hoof and the whole lamb moved stiffly. He buried the four of them in a post-hole for the shed, and tried to comfort his wife; but she was sullen.

After lunch she said in the precise clipped tones of her mother, "Where are you going, John?"

"To the paddocks, Jo,"

"What about the shed?"

"The shed. Don't you realize, Jo: out there there's a ewe going down every quarter hour. Look at the crows."

"That's all very well," Jo said in a hard voice. "But I've got to have some place to live."

Clement dug his heels into his horse's flanks and galloped down the slope into the valley. When he returned after dark, Jo was dressed in her new silk dress.

"I'm sorry, John," she said. "I was a bitch."

The lights were back in her hair, the hut looked the way it used to look and a cocktail jug and two glasses were on the small curved antique table between their chairs.

"I thought we might go to town for dinner," Jo said. "I'd like to."

"Jo, it's late," Clement said. He threw his hat into the corner and slumped down into a chair still wearing his greatcoat. Running his fingers through his hair, he could smell the smell of ewe-flesh. "And I'm dog tired, Jo. I've got to be back in the paddocks early tomorrow."

He looked up from unlacing his boots and saw a ghost of the morning beneath the soft powders and rouge on his wife's bright face.

"Have a drink," she said.

She had mixed four of gin to one of vermouth.

Sitting in the lounge of the Commercial, waiting for more drinks after dinner, his arms along the hard crescent arms of the bucket chair, wanting another drink and feeling the excitement leak out of him like the dribble of beer over the edge of the ring-stained table, Clement leaned over and took his wife's hand. He smiled at her and said, "You're enjoying yourself, aren't you, Jo?"

And meeting her eyes, his excitement returned on a wave of tenderness.

"You're the only girl for me, Jo," he said. "You make this place seem like Princes. I'd like to dance, wouldn't you?"

"Look at that woman's hat," Jo said. "John, you wouldn't believe it."

"Look away, quick," Clement said. "He's coming over."

187

The heavy, mild countryman pursing over coffee with the woman, had risen and was riding-off chairs towards them.

"You're John Clement," he said. His handshake was firm like a grip on reins, and his eyes were mild and direct. "I met you at the last sheep sale. My wife and I were wondering if you'd join us for coffee?"

"Unfortunately," Clement said rising. He introduced Jo.

"Wilton," the man nodded. "Peter Wilton."

"Unfortunately, Mr. Wilton, we've ordered coffee already."

Clement kept his eyes firmly on Jo.

"Well, that's all right. I'll tell the waiter to bring it over."

"We'd love to," Jo said.

Clement walked over to the other table still looking at his wife.

"A hard season," Wilton nodded. He crossed heavy thighs and turned sideways towards Clement as if still in the saddle, talking through cigarette smoke. His eyes looked through the smoke, long-sighted and kind. "You're unlucky to strike it like this your first year." He pulled at the knee of his trousers, watching the smoke rise. "We're having some trouble with the lambing, over our way. How's yours going?"

"No trouble," Clement said. "None at all. Not a bit."

The bastard, he thought. He's engaging me in conversation. Mrs. Wilton was looking at Jo from under her hat and asking her if she kept fowls.

"Then you're lucky," Wilton said, looking at Clement. He had thought him a decent young man.

"I expect it's all a matter of management." Clement said. And he met Wilton's eye.

Mrs. Wilton sat forward when she heard the change in her husband's voice, a plain tired nervous woman who found conversation difficult, and talked too much. She smiled through and beyond Clement and fluttered her gloves. The hat sat over one eye.

"I was just asking Mrs. Clement if she kept fowls," she said.

"No," said Clement. "But she's jealous of a fox."

And suddenly sick of himself, he said, "Excuse me, please," and walked out into the hall. As he left he heard Mrs. Wilton say, "Jealous of a fox! What a curious thing to say! Oh, I see." And she began to laugh.

In the hall he bought the morning paper from a woman behind the desk. He took the paper, paused, and said, "Never trust a man with blue eyes."

"You've got blue eyes yourself," the woman said.

"Never trust him."

He gave the woman two shillings and walked into the reading room muttering: "There you are: pots of dough: money to burn! Just paid two shillings for a paper."

In a deep chair he spread out the paper, closed one eye, and said, "Tricked you that time, didn't I." The double lines of print had converged.

Reading the headlines with one eye, he speculated on the possibility of another war. He wondered what Jo had done with his uniforms.

"They're doing very nicely," he said to Jo over the paper when she came in.

"John, what are you talking about? I've been looking for you everywhere. You've insulted Mr. Wilton who's nice, and kind. And what a silly thing to say about that fox."

189

She was flushed and angry.

"I'm sorry Jo. Really I am. I didn't mean a thing." And he drew her down towards him. "Let's not fight. It was just, well, we'd been having a good time. And do you know what Wilton said to me?" He began to laugh. "He asked me if I was having any trouble with my sheep."

"Don't John," Jo said. She was sitting on the arm of the chair smoothing his hair. "Do you know what the Hat asked me? She asked me if I was having a baby."

Clement sprang forward to the edge of the chair and said, "There you are! That's just it. You can't put up with it."

Then shutting one eye and frowning, gauging, troubled, he said, "You're not having a baby, are you Jo? You're getting a bit of a pot, you know. You're not having a baby, are you Jo?"

"You don't want one, do you John?"

Jo was smoothing his hair.

"No," he said.

"Then I'm not having one. You know I'd do anything for you, John."

"All this talk about babies," Clement said. "We must keep away from those Wiltons. Let's have a drink. No, give me a kiss." And he pulled her down into the chair.

"No, not here John. Hat might come in."

"Then in the car."

And they got up and walked out under the steel light of the neon over the street door.

The next morning Clement was late getting out into the paddocks. There was a fog, heavy and woollen, and occasionally a corner of fog would lift revealing an acre of white ground, the white trees, and logs cast like sheep, in a fur of frost. The fog was cold with the cry of crows and, in the rifts, Clement could see their black wings beating the mist.

It was his worst morning so far. He stumbled on six crow-torn ewes, and skinning them, running the knife cleanly down the insides of their legs, and feeling other knives under his fingernails, he thought that it was very like war. You were frightened the first few days and then you got used to it. But if you had a break and came back to it, it was like starting all over again.

While he was skinning the last ewe, the mist swirled and lifted. And there in the gap, on the stone hillside, was the fox. It was crouched over the dead body of a lamb in much the same attitude as he was bending over the carcass of the ewe. And as the gap widened, it raised its head and looked at him. Clement noticed that the trunks of the trees that had been gold in summer, had paled to grey and were stained with crimson on their windward side. Then the mist flapped down again.

He rode home for breakfast and found that Jo was having trouble with the stove. She was excited and nervous.

"Six of 'em this morning," he said, "torn to bits by crows. And how many more under this fog, I don't know."

"Don't tell me about them. Don't tell me. I don't want to know."

There was a wild light of fear in her brown eyes.

To change the subject, Clement said, "I saw that fox this morning. It had killed a lamb."

"What did I tell you!" Jo said. "There you are!" She was standing over the cold stove and her eyes were unnaturally bright. There was a shrill note of despair in her voice, despair and triumph. Clement noticed again the heaviness of her body. "There, I told you."

"You told me nothing." Clement said.

After breakfast he took down the rifle and rode out across the valley. The fog had lifted and hung in a steel dome over the hill. Beneath it, crows flew in loose scattered formations, winging down into the grey trees.

Halfway up the hill, a ewe had just gone down. She had a lamb half-delivered and crows sat in a patient ring around her. Clement took the lamb by its forelegs and dragged it from the ewe's belly, warm and yellow and living, and slapped its thin chest until it staggered up among the sticks and leaves. He walked the ewe until she could stand, sat her down and placed the lamb under her neck. When the ewe began licking the lamb, he knew that everything was all right.

He left his horse on the hillside and clambered up the crest on foot. A deep gully scarred the weather side, and he saw the fox loping up the gully between the yellow-box roots, trailing its brush, its sharp nose lowered towards the sheep-pad. Every now and then the fox paused, listening, scenting the one mile wind.

Clement followed it with the rifle, and when it paused the next time, he fired.

The fox shied up the bank, sneering back its lips, and came on up the hill. It galloped suddenly at right angles between the stones, and paused. It had not seen Clement. Clement fired again, hearing the soft pulpy thud of the bullet. The fox clawed itself over a boulder, dragging the weight of its body along with its forepaws. Its lips were drawn back in a smile of pain.

Clement ran out from behind the brushwood and found the fox rolled over, showing a long scarf of white down the front of its body. He saw the crimson froth spreading out and the darker blood overflowing it and staining the frost. And all the exhilaration went out of him.

192

He sat down on the boulder beside the fox and felt the warmth of its body, as it cooled and stiffened.

Below, above the dead grip of the frost, crows were flying; and a magpie alighted into wind and stepped in carefully on stick legs to peck at the carcass of a ewe.

He sat there for some time, looking down, and feeling the rising of the wind. And then he saw the lambs playing.

There were twenty of them together around a fallen tree, and they were using it as a springboard. They would run up the log and prop and half turn back; and leap in turning, high, to land stiff-jointed on the desolate ground; playing while the ewes grazed the frost and the wind blew with the first bitterness of spring.

Clement rode on around his sheep while the wind broke up the sky, trailing gigantic shadows.